2018

MINDFEEDER+
Restoration

Written By:
Ciara J Swan

Printed in the United States of America

ISBN: 978-1-732-60580-0
LCCN: 2018913608

Book design by Create Space
Cover design by Ciara J. Swan
Cover illustration by Ciara J. Swan

Published by Ciara J. Swan

To my loved ones, we are blessed in emotional, mental, physical and spiritual abundance. We are nourished and provide a constant source of nourishment. We are healers. We are healed.

Lord, Creator, Most High, Most Low, Most Present, empower our actions and thoughts to serve the betterment of our being as individuals and collective forces. Keep us grounded in peace, keep us lifted in grace.

Smelly Digest
Scene 1

The stage is set with a box. Inside the box, there is a room with a bed, desk and chair. There is one window. The gloss of the moon outside the window captivates the body, drenched in a pool of sweat. The body insistently stares in awe and suddenly clenches its stomach, from the stomach its mouth, from the mouth its forehead. The body flings forward in one of those exorcist contortions, leaving a trail of water while leaping to the desk and chair at its left. The body now stationed in a 90-degree posture, is hanging onto the cramps of stomach and mind. Blood flows with a godly force down the well of womb and streams along their thighs. Black body, waits in moisture.

(This is the state of a body who is rotting with sweetness. days pass and this self-banter continues)

Black body shines with a particular luminescence; that of encrusted golds, coppers and honeys. For 24 days and 23 nights, this body rekindles traumas through kundalini poses:

Elongation of neck, expansion of arms, plank-aviation of legs; flight and fire breaths

"What is healing?" Black body whispers to itself, back crooked and contemplating pains of past lives. The same ache that plagued its stomach, now crept up the spine and rests comfortably at body's neck. Involuntary muscle spasms follow.

"Adaptable endurance," a calm voice responds after careful consideration. Black body now assured of their hysteria, laughs uncontrollably until their abdomen tightens.

"How does one endure inequity?" Black body challenges omniscience.

"Like rivers, we must ebb and flow, it is not enough to be still." Black body shifts upright, legs and feet overlapping the other. They sit in cyclic thought, digging unkempt fingernails into flesh, before attempting a remark.

"What's happening to me? My menstruation has lasted for several weeks now and I am emitting a pungent odor"

"You are awakening"

"From-"

"Idle slumber"

"Solitude…"

"Hyper-sensitivity; your suffering from a bout of anxiety induced a plethora of bodily responses. Overwhelming isn't it? -

it's amazing the number of strengths you've accumulated in such a short time"

"It's been shy of a month"

"You've been unconsciously practicing all of your life"

(Scene Fades out)

Scene 2

(One of the neighbors inside the cubicle compound overhears citronella talking to herself for weeks and finally decides to call the Psyche Spirit's office)

Neighbor:
Hey uhh, can you get someone over to Oaktron Mirage Complex, there seems to be a 24/7 happening in Compound 53, this lady is off her jets, she keeps gasping, I hope she's not in danger...please send help!

Receptionist:
Sure, I'm sending some controllers now. Can you go outside of her door and report the odor? Maybe I can do some preliminary trouble shooting over the phone

Neighbor:
Hold on

(The neighbor hovers over to Citronella's front door and places their nose against the screen door)

Hey spirit, it smells like soiled roses and seaweed

Receptionist:
Is it more earthy or oceanic?

Neighbor:
If I had to choose, I guess oceanic: salty

Receptionist:
Hm, we updated all Miragian servers this past season.
The sea setting was merely a test to gauge our
efficiency in large bodies of water. Alright many
thanks. I'll send some controllers over there shortly,
hopefully you can get some rest, in spite of the noise.
I advise you to stay away from her compound, she
could be a threat.

*(The neighbor disconnects contact and goes back to
cubicle 53 and pounds on Citronella's door)*

Neighbor:
Uh…miss

Knock, Knock

Neighbor:
Excuse me, miss! I hope you're alright. I called the
Psyche Spirit and their sending some Controllers over
now

*(The neighbor presses their ear to the door and
listens for any sign of commotion. On the other side
of the door, Citronella fumbles for her sanity and
tries to tidy her living arrangement)*

Citronella:
Is this your idea of an awakening? Now folks think
I'm talking to myself!

*(Citronella slips over some soiled clothes from yester
night and staggers to turn off the lights before*

entering her bedroom closet. She waits and nervously chews the skin around her fingertips)

Scene 3

(Controllers fire gaze Citronella's front door to ashes and search her cubicle compound. Pots of spoiled fruit and jars of soaked flowers were scattered throughout each corner of her cubicle compound)

Controller 2:
510, come in Psyche Spirit, code 510. It's a messy situation, seems like a native lives here.

Psyche Spirit:
How can you tell?

Controller 2:
Signs of sacred practice scattered about the cubicle, everything is soaked, the water comes up to our ankles

Controller 1:
Hey, I heard something coming from the cubicle compound's rear

(Both Controllers, careful of their footsteps, venture west of the compound. Controller 1 prepares retinal intuition and peers through each closed door)

Controller 1:
Check this out deuce!

(Controller 1 crouches down and presses into the floor)

Controller 1:
It appears to be a trail of blood

(Controller 2 follows the trail to the bedroom closet)

Controller 2:
Copy, calling Psyche Spirit, Come in Psyche Spirit, we've located the subject

(Both Controllers reach into the closet and drag Citronella out)

Controller 2:
She's fully dressed, no signs of self-abuse but she's mumbling to herself. We can't make out the language

Psyche Spirit:
Copy. Controllers please refrain from rough handling, give her the vaccine and report to the lab

Controller 2:
Copy

Scene 4

(Citronella rises up to a throbbing bruise on her upper right arm. She looks down at it and notices a coin sized blister bubbling with pus. She immediately panics. She tries to get up and run but falls over a touch screen monitor. She looks around, there is only one operating table amidst the foggy purple room)

Nostalgia:
They've got you figured out now

(Spurts of blood coughed from Citronella's vagina)

Citronella:
Who in the world is that?

Nostalgia:
Im down here

(Citronella now feeling the vibrations of the voice at her womb, looks down; jaw gaping)

Citronella:
But that's impo-

Nostalgia:
Ah, ah, careful, don't say something that's obviously not true

(Blood squirts from her womb)

Citronella:
But how am I bleeding? My cycle is not due for
another few weeks

Nostalgia:
Listen closely, there's a war going on outside of your
thighs. Your blood is a symbol of their presence.
Every time an outsider, who is hazardous to our
survival is near, we bleed

Citronella:
What war!? Theres no war in the Oaktron Mirage
Complex District. Theres nothing wrong with me.
Theres no war. What do you mean I'm a target?

Nostalgia:
You are right child, there is nothing wrong with you.
In fact, everything in your right, is what's wrong.
You have something the multiverse has lost; the
ability to portate. You would have gone unnoticed if
it weren't for your meddling neighbor.

Citronella:
You've got to be kidding me

Nostalgia:
To be honest, I don't know what the ancestors saw in
you. You complain, you self-deprecate, you mock
your own gifts

Citronella:
Everyone has psychical abilities in Mirage

Nostalgia:
But everyone needed the vaccine, you were born with it

(*Citronella yanks the intravenous solution from her forearm and fumbles around the purple lit room, feeling the surface of the floor bed, she finds a crack in the tile. Seconds later, Controllers march into the operating room with blankets and needles in their hands*)

Controller 1:
Stand up now and undress yourself

Citronella:
Why are you doing this? Who are you?

Controller 2:
Do not resist!

Controller 1:
She's bleeding, we need back up towels in here

(*Citronella was placed firmly onto the operating table, legs spread a part. Before the Controllers could ply the mirror to her vagina, she kicks one of them and grabs the needle from the other. She leaps at the Controller on the floor and plunges the needle into their neck. The second Controller charges after her; staggering, she forces the broken piece of tile from the floor bed and jams it into the Controllers' kneecap. Citronella makes for the door. The hallways are dim, but she sees a glowing light to her right and runs toward it)*

Controller 2:
Security Unit come in, I repeat, Security Unit please come in…Do you copy?

Security Unit:
Copy, this is Security Unit 6

Controller 2:
Subject C-87-2053 has escaped the Operating Unit, we need a lock down

Nostalgia:
I told you they were near…you mustn't get too comfortable, this portal will eventually run out of time

Citronella:
Who are they? – A portal?

Nostalgia:
MindFeeders, those Controllers are only guinea pigs for the Psyche Spirit. She knows about the 14-year cycle and preys on women with our gift

Citronella:
What cycle? What gift!? It feels like a curse…

Nostalgia:
You know that smell you keep emitting. It is not human. It connects you to a sea tribe

Citronella:
But I'm an insect, a product of Mirage

Nostalgia:
You must unlearn what has been programmed. The MindFeeders have spent generations priming complete populations to believe they are inadequate, unable to thrive without the Alphacorp support

Citronella:
They gave me something, it's in my arm, it feels like it's spreading!

Nostalgia:
They took your samples and injected cerebral anesthesia

Citronella:
How do you know all of this?

Nostalgia:
Because while you are asleep, I am aware. Your conditioning does not travel to me, you only have 20 minutes remaining until the portal deactivates

Citronella:
What can I do?

Nostalgia:
Rub me and find your answers

Citronella:
You want me to masturbate?

Nostalgia:
Your property needs to be replenished. You must act
quickly.

(*Citronella began rubbing Nostalgia. 21 eye blinks
pass, Nostalgia purrs with each stroke and squirts
blood. A tiny piece of copper wire appeared in
Citronella's bloodied hand*)

Nostalgia:
Stick this wire into the back of your neck, now

Citronella:
But wh-

Nostalgia:
Now!

(*Citronella stabs the wire into the back of her neck
and waits, five eye blinks*)

Nostalgia:
Your body will now take you back in time. Back to
the onset of your bromidrosiphobia. The Controllers
released a community wide vaccine that leached onto
foreign agents and produced counter-effects. This
explains your sudden episodes of hyper excrement
emittance; your spirit is dehydrated. Fortunately,
because you are not a true Miragian, you felt those
side-effects and underwent gradual suffering. You
need to figure out a method to cure your negative
reaction. During this time travel, you must remember
your true form...

Citronella:
I…I don't remember taking a vaccine and what do you mean my truest form?

Nostalgia:
I cannot give you more info Citronella, please remember for the sake of saving yourself-
Go back…

(*As Citronella focuses on her breathing with Nostalgia's voice guiding her, the copper wire in the back of her neck begins to send tingling waves up and down her vertebral column. The surrounding objects in the room begin to fade and nostalgia's voice muffles*)

Nostalgia: Go back!...

Scene 5

E:
Get your insect repellant! Come and get it! Fresh out the mixer

Y:
We've got Jasmine Blossom, Sunflower Zest, Same Ol' Shit, E'stranged Fruit and so much more!

E:
Are you in need of a makeover? Does your operating system freeze? You've come to the right place!

(Citronella found herself in the middle of a jam-packed Town Market, vendors and buyers swarmed in every crevice. The smell of smoked fish and burning plastic invaded her senses. Intrigued by the tone of these eager insects, she managed through the crowd and approached them)

C:
What exactly does this repellant, repel?

E:
You got this one Yael?

Y:
Yea, I'll take it from here
You ever get those annoying glitches in your third-dreyeve? Does it ever beep monotonously and flash dull colors? Well this *(holds up repellant)* is like gold

at the end of a rainbow. You never see it, but know it's there…

C:
Wait, so why all the names?

Y:
Well, uhh…we figure, if we can locate all the senses that belong to each insect, carefully bottle them and package it for consumption-

E:
What my colleague is trying to say, ma'am, is that there can be no glitch in any insect's system if they can excrete multiple instinctual senses at once

C:
Im so lost…

E:
No ma'am, *space is the…*

Y:
Place! Let's take a look at your system

(*Citronella reluctantly squats revealing six openings to her system*)

Hmm… She's a 92

(*Today's models have more than twelve sensory points*)

Your software is considerably outdated, it's a
blessing you survived without a crash

E:
Alright, what do we have here? Usually, outdated
systems have at least five sensory points. Yet your
system is only displaying two active senses; smell
and taste. Both sensory points seem to denote
heightened awareness in oceanic environments

*(After a few moments of quizzicality, Ethera
whispered into his right cuff link)*

E:
Have you been experiencing any symptoms?

C:
Just some typical night sweats

Y:
It seems like you still have a collar, would you like to
deactivate it?

(Citronella hesitated for quite some time)

Ma'am I can sense your uneasiness, but many of the
insects today do not have collars, that additional
firewall security is no longer needed

C:
If you think it's a good idea... how long does the
download take?

Y:
Seven eye blinks

(*One...*)

E:
Yael, take samples of both sensory points and stores
them for crash course testing

Y:
Got it boss

(*Yael carefully swipes bio degradable gauze over
each sensor*)

(*Three...*)

C:
W-wait, I didn't give consent to upgrade my third-
dreyeve!

(*Citronella tries to push Yael off of her*)

Y:
Ma'am, we are actually doing you a service. If any
MindFeeders working for the Psyche Spirit notice an
imbalance in your system, you could be subjected to
cruel punishments or worse

C:
Is there a way to preserve my '92 framework? Some
backup disk or junk drive that can be accessed at the
onset of identity loss?

E:
It seems, Citronella, like you know what you need.
Unfortunately for you, this is an era of want

C:
Ethera, is it?

E:
Yes, ma'am

C:
Well, Ethera, Im asking because I know how shaky
the newer models are. Flighty Fellows. I need my
constancy and what if there is a glitch along the way?

Y:
Change is constant Citronella

E:
Ahh, don't get too righteous Yael

(*Citronella cooled from her hysteric angst*)

C:
No, no, it's allowed. See, how can you be a good
salesman and not know how to pitch? I'm just
looking for additional security

(*Seven...*
Ethera tapped the nape of her neck and sent her body
into paralysis)

E:
Very well, before finalizing your upgrade, we will make second scans of your system. They can only be stored at room temperature for ten years. Thereafter, it can be frozen for twenty years. If you want to revert to your old operating system, you must ingest the perishable file on an empty stomach

(*He tapped her neck once more after dragging the files*)

C:
Whew! So, I have thirty years' time?…I'm a little dizzy

E:
From this day forward, you have twelve smells and six you can access within a thirty-blink window

Y:
Eighteen senses in total. Here is your old identity. You cannot download another copy

(*Yael handed Citronella her old self, packaged neatly, in a glycerin capsule…*

Ethera carefully hovered both hands over Citronella's neck, his antennae slowly crept from the crown of his head, as ultra-violet waves seeped from his palm exposing her electro-magnetic collar)

E:
It seems like it'll take more than an upgrade to get your collar off...are you sure you're a true Miragian?

C:
What constitutes a true Miragian?

E:
The ability to absorb systemic conditioning. Your third-dreyeve almost rejected our updates

(*Ethera hovered his right hand over Citronella once more and noticed abrasions along her neck, arms, and back*)

E:
What are these?

(*Citronella cupped the front of her neck and remembered her womb's words, "go back"...*)

C:
Can I still function?

E:
At your leisure

Y:
Oh ma'am, do be careful on how you navigate your new system. You may attract some insects you don't want

C:
Than how is it a repellant?

Y:
Traditionally, repellant is used to ward insects off.
But today's models have adopted a 'sway' function.
To sway, means that the repellant can attract or
distract another.

E:
Because most models can now access a myriad of
aromas, many insects possess sensoric immunity

Y:
It took some time Ms. Citronella, but we've managed
to tweak a few of your cellular structures. Your collar
is now deactivated, and your system is up to date

C:
Something doesn't feel right…

(*But before Citronella could confront the eager
salesmen, they evaporated, leaving behind a strong
putrid odor. Bouts of static interrupted her
subconscious thoughts as she wandered around the
lonely city. Citronella knew that only minutes
remained before a portal would reappear and she
had yet to remember her full essence or how they
blocked her senses. An oil-stained newspaper
manifests at her right foot. On the front page, she
sees a group of radical appearing females and the
words Agri-Pus Connection, sprawled across. One
female elder stood out from the rest; tentacles*

covered her face and branch like scars outlined her copper skin. For a split second, Citronella feels a wave of deja-vu and a purple beam ascends from the center of the newspaper creating a magnetic spiral

Poof!

They found me unconscious, my bruised skin covered in jasmine blossoms. For weeks, I was questioned about a place called 'home'. Once they realized my ineptitude in answering their questions of my origin, the physical beatings stopped. First, I cried, bit through the flesh of my bottom lip until the blood pouring tasted like a ripened cherry; mechanizing my pain. I was force fed through tubes, for 22 days, somehow they sensed the value of my being and deemed me indisposable. After a month of mutism, I uttered the sequence, "C-87-2053," which I repeated hours on end, until the sequence became incoherent. Those hysterical episodes empowered them to initiate a series of physically and psychically laborious tests, it was then that my regard for nature was acknowledged.

Often, I'd rise from a deep sleep with new scars on my body. Weeks of experimentation passed, and I noticed an incremental numbing sensation at the base of my genitalia, followed by coughing sounds. I tried my best to ignore the pulsating murmurs of my vagina, until I finally caved into the psycho-somatic needs and began a dialogue with her. Before her, time was irrelevant, the totality of my being, while conscious, was spent staring at walls and piecing residual memories. Involuntary solitude brought out my inner spirit. I was transferred to the Agri-Pus Plant, once they discovered me talking to myself. It wasn't hard acquiescing since the majority of prisoners were colorful wombs fulfilling life long sentences of servitude.

"Are you Queer yet?" a voice slurred, a bullet of saliva followed and hit my left eyelid.

"What do you mean, 'Queer'?" I questioned.

"Most, if not all, of the wombs here at Agri-Pus Plant, have been given life sentences for their radical sexual beliefs and cravings. We were exiled from our communities when we failed to adhere to the Alphacorp doctrine *of feeding, financing and fucking* men. We opted to do all of that on our own and created a Co-Op out of our immeasurable terms." They waited for a response.

"Sounds like you got a good bargain, I barely knew who I was before they shipped me here," I tried to compost my sarcasm. "Can you point me in the direction of Compound 92?" After moments of directional cues and before they could manage more conversation, I sped off to my lodging.

Revelations experienced through consistent bouts of anxiety

There is a socio-politic warfare quaking betwixt my thighs, I call her, Nostalgia. She foundations the root of blood and seed. She is co-adaptor and sole cultivator of born life. She is black, she is bottomless, she is whole, synonymous to a star enveloping itself. On the first or third day of every month she can be heard spitting, "Revolution!" between spurts of sacrificed blood. She knows not how to control these rhythmic regularities, and so the seeds drop leaving my black body to cultivate such a cosmic knowledge. Sometimes, when I can't seem to form the words audibly, I write letters to her and squat over them during menstruation:

> Nostalgia,
>
> The sun and moon can be found shivering, naked, in my desolate moistness. I did not choose this life; to be an extension of the physical body that houses me. I am sacred, my scars do not scare me | I am temple, my feet are the roots to my mind | I am sacred temple, my scars accentuate my roots | I am healing, *we* are *forever* healing
>
> Learning Love,
>
> A Bitter Black Body

The blood falls at random, highlighting specific words in scarlet; I hold these words to be ceremonial truths and recite them repetitively.

and/life/extension/scars/temple/my/Learning/Black.
And/life/extension/scars/temple/my/Learning/Black

In spite of Agri-Pus Plant being an accommodating space filled with queer wombs, there was still the underlying fact of it being an internment sentence. Three years passed like perspiring leaves at dawn and a perpetual boredom made up the entirety of my being. In spite of the angst, I managed to make a comfortable living here. The sequence, "C-87-2053," kept plaguing my mind and something reminiscent of despair, ached inside of me. No herbal blend could ease the pain of mentally and physically taxing labor. My black skin had already been a home for disgruntled and well-advised foremothers; muscle and emotional spasms carried from past generations infused with my own quarrels conditioned a peculiarity within.

The walls unlike those in my prior captivity, are made of red clay. The red reminded me of an earth I had long since touched. I tried my best to preserve my growing consciousness of Nostalgia in ritual confinement but news spread like wildfires and folks were waiting for a new pariah. The validity of Nostalgia was obsolete for this small town. Since most of the days were spent around glossy, cool stares and conspicuous gossip, nights of solitude were warmer.

Another long day of work under the probing sun without proper nourishment and hydration, left Body drearily drudging, cotton mouthed and heavy hooved to their compound. Once home and slightly replenished, body strains itself in front of a cracked mirror and calls to her fairy womb

"Nostalgia, we are alone now..."

"Be it the wiz who dumb, dome founded in foolish glory," Nostalgia spits for her wandering owner to practice more intentional conjuring.

"You're babbling that blood talk again?"

"It seems like you've lost your soul connection, the spirit which drives you."

"Spirit has no dealings in this situation," body chuckles sarcastically.

"Watch your mouth, body."

"Stalg, we've been tuning this same record for years and nothing has changed. We've tried it all!"

"Surely not *all* YOU could…" Nostalgia challenges.

Body fills a pitcher and steps outside to water her plants. She is bare underneath a tethered pair of blue corduroy overalls, she gently squats to water a plot of lilacs and hums, "summer breeze," a tune her foremothers carried for 8 generations. Although Body could recall 700 years of her familial bloodline, she couldn't recollect why or how she transferred from Oaktron Mirage to Agri-Pus. The strain kept her brows furrowed until a black butterfly traipsed amidst the raspberry sorbet sky and landed smack dab on her right corduroy thigh; circling itself.

"Well it seems mama nature disagrees with your ill claim," Nostalgia sends an aching pulse through body's root, "we need balance." The knock at Body's womb shifted her to the right. She gripped her stomach with an unyielding force and sucked her teeth; reasoning to catch the calibrated breath Nostalgia misplaced for her to find.

"I have lit seven-day candles, burnt sacred woods and herbs to the ancestors, meditated on earth's crystals…and still I ache," Body fell plump on her ass.

"Spiritual practice is only enough when the self is fully invested…enough of that, we got tunnels to dig and branches that need hydrating," Nostalgia mutters spasmodically.

"For the past week, you've instructed me to fetch a gallon from the outsource pipeline and drink it before sunset," body fails to laugh at the absurdity, "we don't want to drown and folks around here are starting to commit themselves to my business."

"Well the way you're moping around, it seems there's a drought and don't mind the others."

"You know Stalg, it's like I'm a slave around here, just an idle thing in the presence of your holiness. The body is supposed to be the master, controlling, making us function."

"I would not be here, had you known how to use your power."

"How do you figure Im not myself?" I ask, not truly waiting for an answer.

"Because you don't pray to me like you use to, rub me after a long day of work, or remember to plant our scarlet offerings to the weeds."

"I've been tired, womb."

"There is a magnetism in your slumber, black, the more you drift from your-"

"I thought we had tunnels to dig and branches to hydrate?"

"I reckon you are right miss body, there is work to do and work can't be done-"

"*If our properties aren't properly replenished,*" body aids in chorus to Nostalgia's sermon.

"One last thing Body, there's a force approaching you. Be wary because when you cross paths, your course of life will change."

"Stalg, can I ask you something?"

"Homesick in your own skin? As thoughts manifest themselves into words, you will have your answer."

It must be noted that Nostalgia, as an extension of Body's root, innerstands Body's feelings even before she does. Most ailments; of cerebral, intestinal or spiritual functions are connected. The neurons transmit messages constantly and Nostalgia being at Body's diaphragm, gets tuned to both ends.

"From my very beginning, there has been a pain that seems to culminate from the excavation of womb to the darkness of heart, but there is no blood."

"Child, pain only transcribes itself as trouble, if work has been left undone. That ache you feel has more to do with you unfulfilling your destiny than an actual wound. You are first a seed before a body, what do seeds require?"

"Water..."

"Correct...if you do not properly nourish the seed that is your body, you will never germinate into your full being."

Nostalgia placed a careful burden on Body's mind, which took the form of sinus pressure that forced her to excrete the destructive forces from within. Phlegm filled fantasies.
Still outside, Body decides to start supper and peeled some fresh cassava root and plantains she had bought from another convict the day prior. Oil cracked atop the creased finishes of her brown dermis; she never flinched.
Belly full and mind bare, body takes a scorching hot shower. 150 eye blinks pass.

The steam gradually cleared from the restroom and a cool fell over spreading goosebumps over the naked body

"Practice worshipping your pain."

"Worship my pain…being okay with it?"

"No, baby, being okay with the scars. Sadly, our culture glorifies pain. The self, craves this form of despair, to blame an external force but you need to fix an internal problem."

"But Nostalgia, Mother and Elder, I am tired of feeling this ache. It is constant, it is relative."

"There is inequity somewhere…perhaps the enactment of change in your personhood is nearing. Move with the feather gravity and the darkness of light. My love, it seeps from your melanin, these stars envelop themselves just to reach you. What are you truly afraid of, your own wings?"

"Who am I to diminish my own actuality? A drone, a robot, a time bomb waiting to cause cultural deficit? A mindless wanderer, a passer of time, a person who only has enough courage to take what has been allotted? A dream, an object, a subject, a spectacle of black matter, something wanton, something dis-abled and dis-eased…I am not a teacher, I have not been healed."

"You are circling as beautifully as the black butterfly who greeted you this evening. Self-deprecation does not suit you, my dear. It is obvious you're mindful, it is not clear your disposition, when you seem to emit answer from your own skepticism."

"These wings you speak of, where can I find them?"

"In language, in God; create your potions, tabernacle a rhythm and unearth the clues. A force is coming…A force is coming…"

Body and Nostalgia walk through the cannabis field about 800 feet until they reach the main building. Although Nostalgia is too, a being, the exterior world can only see and hear Body. As Body entered staff quarters for check-in, she heard neighboring co-workers mutter hear-say about her spells:

"Why she always looking to the earth under her?" one asked, and the other attempted to reason, "probably whispering to the spirit."

Whenever Body's eyes met theirs, they would scurry to the sky or through Body's soul, like she wasn't even breathing the same air. This particular tom-foolery didn't faze Body because she understood the overwhelming ailments of this era; ignorance. Nostalgia had coached her before on turning a blind eye to the negated forces with*out*; the power to understand the truth with*in*.

At that exact moment when Body remembered to breathe deeply and reject social nuances, the two walk over to the central computing system where Body was scanning her fingerprints for the day's shift.

"Say, you the one folks call, Spirit Whisperer, huh?" The stalky one asked only long enough to hear her own response, "I mean, is it true you go 'round tappin' tunes with higher forces?"

"Now don't go ambushing, Phyr!" The second co-worker clears her throat and extends a wrinkled hand,

"Don't mind her, she's not familiar with our ancestor's crafts," flints of gold appeared from her gaping mouth.

"This here is Zephyr, we call her Phyr for short, as you might guess from her personality, and I'm Goldie, if you can't tell by my teeth," Goldie extended her right hand and waited for Citronella to meet her halfway.

"My name is Citronella," she studied the boisterous one over, more carefully, "I don't mind her queries, I don't truly know what to call this gift yet, just *listening*," after speaking her peace, Citronella mirrored Goldie's formal gesture and the two exchanged glimpses of their genetic history through mental images.

"Well I declare! You've got enough stories for the two of our lifetimes combined but you don't speak much," Goldie carefully rolled a leather glove over her right hand and waited for someone to break the silence.

"Well aren't you coy," Phyr added, falling short of Goldie's sincerity, Phyr chimed incessantly, "we never see you 'round much, you got time for us *talking* types?"

Goldie spoke preemptively, "this is Phyr's way of inviting you to our bi-monthly Sister Cypher."

"Na, now don't go deciphering my tongue…what'm saying is, you so busy talking to yourself and those damned plants like you from yonder. Say Goldie, you hear of Special Force trying to find that creature o'here?" Phyr looked Citronella up and down while sucking her teeth. Citronella began to feel uneasy and kept an unwavering stare at Phyr for what seemed like an eternity.

"What are y'all circling around for?" Citronella probed, "besides, it seems like your friend has got me figured out. Citronella continued to transmute Phyr's slick stare.

"Bergamot…Lemongrass…whatever kind of citrus you want to be called, you got something hovering over you- the kind of presence that brings chaos…"

"So why are y'all coming over here, bothering me?" Citronella asked dismissively.

"Pardon my friend, they say opposites attract! Anyway, don't pay her any mind. Sister Cypher is like a conduit for us QPOC," Goldie chuckled on full beam, "you know the spirit shows up in more places than your solitude," Goldie's words seemed to caution.

Citronella tried to conceal her prior dismay of Phyr's accusations and breathed deeply until euphoria swept over her, *phew*! "I hear you," Citronella nodded and held on to their words, as she walked away to the locker room. "Give me the details later, there's work to do! Or have y'all forgot this is a business?" she yelled out. The pair laughed and continued their gossip while Citronella walked toward the locker room.

"The next cypher is tomorrow, after the main shift at 1930 hours. Compound 44!" Goldie flagged Citronella's eyes to meet hers, before resuming her shift. For the first time since her arrival, Citronella felt something outside of herself; a smile crept at the corner of her mouth. Citronella noticed hives rising on her chest while changing into her work clothes and hurried to a mirror. Nostalgia had warned her of ominous irregularities, hours prior, Citronella's mind stretched to a pitch-black room cautioned by an orange light. She stayed on the thought a while longer before returning her attention to the newfound skin tags. "What are you trying to tell me?" She asked aloud. Citronella spent some time researching the braille of her skin. She gathered both her belongings and faculties before heading to the field.

Automatic jet drones flew belligerently above stucco plots and fields, as polyviduals spent their humid dawns forking for stone under richly red soil. White smoke trailed after these sky figures and entire generations remained mindless; the kind of absent mind that spent a lifetime trying to condition itself. Abs contract themselves beneath corrosive flesh with each pull and plunge of worthy biceps; blood, sweat and tears provide offerings to the ancestors.

A salmon haze sprinkled over Citronella's eyelids, as she sun-gazed for a few breaths before resuming her assignment. To any outsider ill-tuned with the laws of land, Citronella was a tree hugger, the type to praise plants and insects. She believed talking to them was part of her success; the plants always seemed to reward her with bountiful shares of herbs and vegetables. Sweat tickled down her forehead and managed to swim its way to the crease of her mouth as she crouched to kiss a small succulent. A shadow slowly crept over her and recalibrated the energy of the late afternoon.

An intrusively eager voice trailed from behind Citronella and brought stale cognac with it, "*Special Force* is arriving soon?" Citronella chuckled without turning toward the unveiled stench, "yea, there's talk about a new immortal genome in our very own backyard." It was Coriander, the lead overseer of the Agri-Pus Plant, who was known for chucking back a few cocktails before, during and after a day's shift. Agri-Pus was the only womb led agricultural collective that cultured medicinal herbs and crops for distribution.

"Well, Nella, you've been here for as long as I've been managing the plot, you know the land inside and out…and…and-"
"Coriander, stammering puts me on edge, just come on with it."

 "Special Force been making threats about shutting down the plant and gutting it to set sights on this organism-"

"And what exactly are you asking of me?"

"To be another pair of eyes and ears for me, I know you've got a testimony, that look in your eyes whenever you touch this land… like you can speak to the soil."

"Damn Cor', where you learn to get deep like that? The liquor preaching to ya now?"

"All jokes aside, Citronella, this is bigger than you and me." Coriander now inched pulses away from Citronella's face, "something's stirring toward us and if you can find the answer before they do-"

"How do you expect me to go out and find some living thing, without knowing what to even look for?"

"Don't get western on me now, like you trained only for the facts. You and me both know this world we living in far from the old country we 'customed to. We're the last of a hue breed and if Special Force finds a greater gene, our kind can be phased out"

"There you go specul-"

"That's a fact for yo ass, Citronella, now what's it gon' be?"

Citronella inhaled deeply to make a conscientious decision, "I'll do my best," she finally exhaled. As if their interaction was her final task, Citronella gathered her gardening tools and retreated to the changing room; along the way, she stared deeply at the surrounding nature, noticing things she had previously neglected. The urgency of a bee's hum, the painstaking joy of a bird's song, the sure bloom of a sprout and vivacity of weeds. Citronella tried her hardest to make peace with the cyclicity of the universe and her part in the whole function.

"We're the last of a hue breed," swirled persistently in Citronella's mind. As much as it pained her, she knew Coriander was right. Each eclipse there was a new micro genocide of the hue breed; mixed descendants of the Afroid Nation. Small pockets of afro-cleansing movements became

normal practices for law enforcement hired by
MindFeeder agent; it wasn't enough to call these acts
of terrorism an albinoid fear of social uprising, it was
merely a game of roulette. Many of the Afroid
revolutionaries and allies were excommunicated and
forced to live the rest of their lives as fleeing outlaws;
disposable.

The Alphacorps hands were becoming
excessively bloodied through spiraling protests cross
continent. Mass depictions of their wicked ways
empowered them to implement safer measures to
extract melanin, via insertable programmed chips into
the pupil. Unfortunately, these were selfish times and
hues could only sympathize with what was spoon fed
to them through mass media coverage, even then, that
wasn't much to keep a pupil's attention. It was rather
easy and strategic for the elite to create another
mechanism to use color as a distraction for classism.
Theories spread about the Alphacorps and their
potential of world dominion, if they were to get
access to a supernatural force. Citronella knew that
research was the only way to find answers about this
new breed and discover why she felt such a strong
connection to something she had never known.

Citronella occasioned the town's library,
after the fourth visit, she resorted to using an alias
once a few clerks questioned her specific title
searches on the afro-indixene tribes remaining in
Agri-Pus. There was hardly any comprehensive
literature of the indigenous hue story, many of the
books within the library database were either checked

out or lost. It was clear then, that Citronella had to use her own gifts which she had long neglected. Nostalgia quivered with excitement once she caught messages from her keeper's conscious. "Is this the work you been trying to get me to do?" Citronella warmly chuckled for Nostalgia to hear. She walked back to her compound, pondering how to contact the remaining elders in their community.

"Stalg, we've been in alignment for years now, how come you haven't taught me how to connect with others like us?"

"You never asked, you were too busy stuck in your-self...our people are never far, Citronella, all you must do is tap into your intentions." For hours, Citronella prayed until salt tears swelled her eyes. She prepared an elaborate meal for her ancestors and placed the red beans and cabbage next to their images on the altar. She waited, drank homemade wine aged in an old cardboard container; dried revelations pouring. The rooster alarmed her as the evening settled into dank soils of the dawn.

"What does Special Force want with this new life force?" Citronella kept repeating the question, each time with more emphasis then the last. She strained her mind to hear the buzzing voices deposit spirit-life game:

> There's a Hue and there's a Man. Hue done been here before, hue listened to folktales and spirituals. Hue learned the teachings and

shared to the group. But Man got the same teachings, listened to the same spirituals and somehow got struck with greed. Man tasted false power and became fearful of losing that dominion, fearful of losing that high…Special Force, is nothing more than a conglomerate of men, parasitic to the innate functioning of any society.

Citronella listened attentively until the ancestors terminated contact, which than made her wonder about the notion of space and time. "What if this new gene is a threat to Special Force's entire structure, I mean why else would they be so adamant on finding this form of life?"

"Citronella, I believe you are finally on to something, for so long, all of hue kind has been castrated, conditioned and ostracized. It is time that we find the nucleus of their weakness."

The sky was purple by the time Citronella was done with her shift. She clocked out at the main office and decided to walk along the riverbank back to the living quarters with her soiled uniform in hand. Along the way she noticed a glow emanating from the east side of the medical plant. It was unlike anything she had ever seen before and somehow, a wave of familiarity drew over her, warming the center of her chest, where the hives rested.

She decided to venture toward the hue, curiosity outweighing fear of the unknown. By the

time Citronella was a thousand feet away, her body
seemed to move involuntarily toward the figure,
tachycardia plagued her as she drew nearer to the
green haze. Each step was met with a queasy gag as
her body tried desperately to repel its radiant force.
Just feet away, she noticed the figure was that of a
naked body surrounded by an emanating light.
Citronella approached with caution; feet first and
torso leant back. Before she could id a particular sex,
she noticed a slippery film coated its body and slid
from its mouth. The radiant body still motionless
allowed Citronella to ease into a squat just above it.
Soft. Murmur. Their chest pointed toward the
caramelized eggplant hue exposing a branded
clavicle. Citronella studied the melanated braille,
with a light graze, and recognized the ancient
indixene symbol of the ocean.

"What are you?" She gasped to herself and gazed
only a while longer before noticing the green layer
covered her palms. Citronella looked at her hands in
disbelief and tried rubbing them together to get the
coat off. However, each stroke of friction acted as a
catalyst and the green film slowly spread from her
hands to her arms. Unbeknownst to Citronella, a
force was created between the two, the green essence
became a magnetic pull, which forced Citronellas
hands to gently massage their frontal lobe. Afraid to
panic, Citronella breathed deeply for some time and
allowed the spiritual happening to go unbothered. As
moments passed, the body levitated and heaved until
their breathing managed to pulsate the gravel beneath
them. A high frequency plagued Citronella's ears as

the immediate earth shook underneath them. An abrupt thud to the ground empowered the being to open their eyes.

"Is this Planet Meditron?" They managed to ask as the green film oozed from their mouth.

"You are in an agricultural province called, Agri-Pus, I do not know this Meditron you speak of." The radiant hue attempted to sit upright but fell victim to gravity's pull.

"We must get there."

"I don't even know your name...get where?" It took Citronella some time to notice that the leafy hue of film resembled blood. It was the kind of blood naked to the human eye, that escaped from the spirit's wound; a happening unseen, only felt. She knew then, that this being was no ordinary spirit. A sharp pain spiraled to the pit of her stomach and caused her to excrete a faint yelp.

"It seems you have no clue of what we are," the body struggled forward and pressed deep into the pit of their wounded abdomen and turned their hand slowly. "Do you feel this?" Citronella churned desperately before gaining governance over her own being.

"Who the fuck are you? How did you-?"

"Citronella, is it? You must find a more effective way of expressing your thoughts…I am your spirit guide."

"I already have one, Nostalgia, she lives in my lap."

"Nostalgia is only a part of your lamented conscious, she is a spiritual agent but she is not your guide. She affirms that your internal needs manifest in the external world."

"So, what is your purpose?" Citronella asked earnestly. They chuckled before continuing, "my purpose is to navigate you closer to your life source…I usually make a more formal appearance," the being gestured to their lack of clothing and pointed to the dirty pair of trousers in Citronella's hands. "Would you mind letting me borrow your garb?" Citronella wearily handed the unknown body her work pants. "Why are you naked?" She tried not to look at the beings genitalia but couldn't help but notice the vaginal labia housed a protruding envelopment like that of an undergrown penis. "Poor manners, have you no shame gawking at another's private areas? Unfortunately, garments and other trinkets that are not necessarily appendages of the body can sometimes be lost during space travel," they smiled.

"Tell me, what is the first thing you think of upon rising?"

Citronella fixed her eyes to the now bone glazed moon, the ivory weaved into a purple dusk and organized her response, "cultivation, it's an overwhelming feeling of desperation, I am both full and empty."

"Fool, is correct! You've been avoiding your greatness, why?"

"I know there is something to be done, I feel that with each bizarre encounter, first Nostalgia…now you…"

"There you go avoiding yourself, it is neither me nor Nostalgia you are afraid of, stop deflecting-"

"I'm unsure of my purpose."

"You truly don't remember who you were before this assignment? The many lives you lived, we've got more work than I thought!" Citronella allowed herself to digest such absolute information from this unknown being, "are you the greater gene Special Force is looking for?"

"Yes, unfortunately, before you found me out in the field, I went through a deal of trouble to locate you. Once we realized your subconscious self, the one you call Nostalgia, could not get through to you, we created a simulation of tests to extract genetic samples from you. It's been 25 years and we are running out of time. Special Force agents were able to track my presence before you did. We need to find a safe place where I can examine your vessel."

Citronella began to walk nervously, her mind raced with all this information. After two miles of inconspicuous crouching, the two found hermitage against tall grass, in viewing distance of her compound. A loud alarm was followed by a monotone voice against an intercom, "this is a reminder, ten minutes before lights out. I repeat, this is a reminder, ten minutes before lights out. All subjects found outside of their respective parameters will be sanctioned to fines."

"Every night, security guards make their rounds to each compound within the 24th hour, if they notice I'm missing, they will shut the plant down"

"I guess this will be your last night in the Agri-Pus Plant, now please, remove your clothing!"

"Look, I know you just miraculously fell from the sky and are unaware of the way things work down here but-"

"Citronella, it will only take me a few scans to determine the cause for your mild memory loss...please, I beg you, we haven't much time to derail the Alphacorps!" The inter-planetary being saw the look of confusion on Citronella's face and reasoned, "I'll explain later!"

"How do you expect me to flail my belongings and strip bare, when I don't even know-"

"Citronella, do you like travelling backwards? Can you not see how bleak our future is?" they heard the confident footsteps of three security guards from 2,000 yards away.

"Honestly, I don't. You've given me no information, I don't even know your name!?"

"I am called, Niamé, and would you please keep your voice down."

"Nee-yah-may...?"

"There will be more time for questions when I figure out what has happened to your Operating System." Citronella slowly removed her clothing and revealed scars that stretched along her clavicle and abdomen.

"Hmm, I figured you would have more scars from humanoid testing, do you remember these scars?"

"They used endoscopes to observe my organ system and implanted medication via feeding tubes- you mentioned earlier that it's been 25 years...what year is it in your multiverse?"

"4020"

"But its 2895 here, in Agri-Pus."

"I am fully aware of our time lapse, Citronella, our existence is multi-dimensional. Time is a mere illusion; you have a genetic copy living in year 2995, both of you are thirty years old and have a passion for herbalism. Have you ever wondered why it seems like gardening is your only mean of survival? It is a trait given from your familial genepool."

Niamé continued to research every fraction of Citronella's body, their unwavering gaze made her cringe back into infancy. At this point, Citronella was past astonishment and could only fix her gaze toward the moon. As Niamé perused Citronella's canvas, they found an irregularity on her right thumb and pressed its mound for several eye-blinks until it caved in. Citronella's entire body went limp as a copper chip protruded from her thumb's nailbed.

"Bingo," Niamé exclaimed monotonously, then inserted the chip into their third-dreyeve. In the beginning, the projections were only distorted images of elders in yellow and blue garments. Niamé's head twitched involuntarily for a while before their body grew lame. While comatose, they tapped into Citronella's recollections and searched for the onset of Citronella's lost powers; royal blue waters and what seemed to be gelatinous nuclei of memorabilia floated along the waves. Niamé reached for the closest memory, their phalanges penetrated through the membrane and accessed the memory:

> Whirling wind | Feather-like tickles tingling skin | Time, turning | Sensation; numb…The sun commands a particular force as insects roam hurriedly through a cluttered marketplace. Images of broken tile and

purple lights swirled inside Niamé's mind. C-87-2053 flashed boldly as they jerked forward from their brief paralysis

It took some time for the mental images to wear off, once their strength was restored, Niamé extracted the chip and positioned it back in Citronella's thumb.

"Usually, uploading information cross third-dreyeves, enable complete access to a hue's recollection. In your case, it seems as though an external user has intentionally placed a blockage. Most of your memories were brief and static-like." Citronella jittered after the hard drive rebooted her mental system.

"Earlier, you told me I have a genetic copy living 100 years in the future, you never told me how or why," Citronella waited for Niamé.
A series of loud banging on Citronella's compound door interrupted the two.

"Citronella! You have 10 eyeblinks to confirm your residency!" The security guard stood alert before kicking her door in, moments later she came out with an article of clothing and held it to the dogs nose for a brief moment, "find her, girl!" The dog excitedly leapt from slumber and made its way toward the open field where the two figures hid.

"I need you to breathe for a moment, this spell requires complete attention."

"A blood thirsty dog is approaching us and you want me to remain calm," Citronella exhaled a shrill cry.

"Breathe in...deeply...allow that focus to guide you to a calm place," once Niamé witnessed Citronella slowly remove her guard, they waved their hands in cyclic motion and an invisibility cloak fell over them.

"Open your eyes and do keep quiet," Niamé hissed in Citronella's ear. As Citronella opened her eyes, the guard dog bum rushed its way through both of their bodies. Citronella looked in disbelief, waxing and waning her hands over her face, "b-but, that's imp-"

"Careful, Citronella, you've realized the idiosyncrasies of this life, we are invisible but they can still hear us." The dog loomed within their presence, sniffing what would have been, their physical bodies. The overweight security guard rushed toward the dog panting, "what you see there fella?"

She removed the flashlight from her hip and scanned the area for remnants of the escapee. Just under the inconspicuous gaze of the security guard and watch dog, Citronella and Niamé moved through the tall, crunchy grass, toward the river bank. The security guard stood in fixed quizzical thought and scanned the area thrice over.

"10-17...We've got a possible missing convict by the name of Citronella."

"10-4, what's your location?"

"I've just arrived at inmate Citron-897's compound.
She's got a nice lil setup here; roses in full bloom,
tomatoes and broccoli sprouting, lavender and
jasmine blossoms hugging the pathway-" Just South
West of Citronella's compound, the officer heard a
muffled noise of what seemed to be like two people
chattering.

"Copy, all units in range, I believe the suspect is on
foot and headed to the river. I heard some voices,"
the guard, still out of breath from her prior sprint did
not wait for the officer to dispatch. She tapped her
right ear and muted the output volume on her
intercom.

"Hey! Is that you Citronella?" She inched closer in
the direction of the muffled sound and whistled for
the k9. Citronella and Niamé, still under guise,
walked slowly toward the river.

"The invisibility spell will wear off once we make
contact with severe elements," Niamé warned
Citronella.

"Let's move faster!" Citronella increased her pace
and just as she was about to step one foot into the
river, Niamé yanked her collar and sent them both to
the ground.

"Citronella, you mustn't move so impulsively, think!
The spell becomes inactive when met with fire, water

and excessive winds. We need to find a stable environment so I can brief you on our journey."

"We will be safer along the water."

"You've never been outside the confines of the Agri-Pus camp, what makes you think you can lead us to refuge?"

"They bring prisoners in by ferry from a central location in the main city, Kampala. The Aruwmi intersects with the Congo River which leads to the Atlantic Ocean... All we have to do is get to Kampala and-"

"How far away are we from Kampala?"

"Under three hours if we hitch a ride."

"Why wouldn't we just take the Nile? It's literally at our feet"

"The waters are too harsh and we have no mode of transportation. Besides, that's what the officers expect from a convict eager to get out of dodge!"

"Just moments ago, you were so willing to jump in the river," Niamé chuckled satirically.

"Your skepticism encouraged my critical thinking. She's getting closer, follow me." They circled around, crept through the high grass and stopped in Citronella's backyard.

"I thought we were trying to get away from this place," Niamé struggled to keep a whispered voice.

"I keep my spare tools buried within my rose bush," Citronella leant over and begun clawing her hands through the hydrated soil. With careful lifting, she uncovered the steel box and opened it to check its contents.

"Ah Ha!," Citronella ecstatically revealed a deeply serrated butcher knife and small .22 caliber.

"What a humanly device," Niamé gagged, "hopefully we won't need those, it's just more weight for this awfully long journey…" Citronella carefully wrapped the weapons in the loose waist folds of her baggy linen trousers and proceeded to crouch through the grass.

"Since you have all the powers, why aren't we teleporting ourselves to safety?" Citronella's voice trailed between sarcasm and irritation.

"Gifts, are privileges and should only be used when necessary," Niamé professed.

"That is precisely why our kind have sustained for so long without succumbing to the tempestuous greed that has plagued many generations."

For hours the two spent time quietly creeping past guards and eventually made their way on the other side of the Agri-Pus' border. Although the night fell over them, they could feel the combination of dirt and sweat hugging their skins.

"Niamé, you never finished telling me about our purpose, who we are, why there are genetic copies of us in alternative spaces…"

"Ah, yes…just before the Alphacorps started their world dominion, a few elders made biological breakthroughs with gene extraction and replication. They used cells from deceased ancestors and noticed that the most regenerative cellular structure was Keratin, which forms naturally in our hair and nails. *Our* elders knew there was an evil keen on degenerating our kind, once they realized that this particular protein was an accumulation of dead cells on the living and transitioned bodies; they began breeding infantile duplicates with heightened gifts."

"Where do the gifts come from?"

"70% of our powers are through prayer, meditation, strict diets and life style choices; the other 30% of them come from ritual initiations passed down by our elders. Most of us who have undergone genetic mutation cannot recall our experiences prior to age ten."

"I always thought something was wrong with me…as if I keep living the same dream over and over," Citronella looked to them in twilight…so, I have powers," Citronella asked naively.

"You are supposed to, they created you to find others like us, cross space-time, to salvage our culture," worrisome swept over Niamé.

"If I have special senses, how could Coriander know of you before me?"

"Someone tapped into your third-dreyeve and rigged your system; while we were in sync, the sequence C-87-2053 kept appearing…" As Niamé recited the coded sequence, Citronella reacted mechanically and jerked at each digit,

"There's something eerie about that code," Citronella stared into the distance for so long, without blinking, that the whites of her eyes seemed to gloss over into the cool black night. Niamé thought she had fallen under another spell and shook her shoulders profusely, "what do you see?"

"Only a flickering purple light."

"I think we are getting closer to your purpose," Niamé stated in subdued revelation. "What did you do with the broken tile?" Her expression turned cold, "there was this stench, looming inside of me; I thought something had rotted, I kept waking each night in pools of sweat…The officers said they wanted to help me, make me better. Once they recognized my apprehension, they labeled me as 'resistant'…started rough-handling me…a-aa-and then they pried my legs open, a wave of adrenaline swept over me. I killed them."

Niamé interrupted, "do not problematize your language and diminish your experience to learned behavior. You protected yourself, how did you escape the operating room?"

"I thought you knew everything, you were sent on this assignment because I failed your mission."

"Just jogging your memory, Nella, we don't believe in failure; only trials and lessons learned. Whoever worked on your third-dreyeve, created some type of fire wall to your memories, without them, it's harder for you to access your true strengths. I can only see as much as you have stored in the very depths of your subconscious. You lack knowledge of self and until our arrival, you were perfectly content with talking to yourself and planting flowers."

"What good would self-hood do if they have us all programmed?"

"My dear, you were never meant to be theirs, you must unlearn docility- how did you escape?"

"A portal," Citronella tried stretching her muscle memory and trailed the nape of her neck, "here!" Citronella whispered to Niamé and directed their toughened hand; the cool sent a numbing sensation across her spinal column. "I've lost most feeling in my back." Niamé breathed deeply and generated energy from their hands and hovered over Citronella's back. Niamé witnessed old accounts of

the abuse she experience through memory and
winced at her pain.

"Your memory of the stinging sensation of each
wound is so vivid," Niamé slowly released their
indifferent shell and a brief moment of concern swept
over their face.

"They are burns."
Niamé spent some time surveying Citronella,
antennae extended from the cleft of their chin and
spread toward Citronella's abrasions, "I am going to
perform an energy dialysis on you, don't be alarmed
by my sensors, they only gravitate to areas of
heightened and stagnant energies. Please breathe
deeply and focus on your thoughts. Now, I need to
know how you managed the copper wire?" a grin
crept on Niame's face.

"Nostalgia, she summoned me to probe her."

"Nostalgia, is a high priestess, who happened to
channel your vaginal walls, you shouldn't mistake
her for *your* genitalia."

"You want me to speak in 'I' statements," Citronella
chuckled foolishly.

"Well, deflecting does no good and only feeds your
illusions-"

"I masturbated and a copper wire appeared in my menses," Citronella retraced the back of her neck before turning to Niamé.

"Was that your first time initiating cervical access?" Niamé asked, aware of the answer. Citronella struggled before answering, "Yes, memories of the Miragian Complex are foggy, I do remember why Nostalgia wanted me to go back"

"Go on…"

"To remember my true form"

"Did you?"

"Not quite, the portal ended before I could retrieve more symbols"

"What was the last thing you saw?"

"A familiar Elder Womb, with tentacles branching from her face"

"Like mine?"

Citronella gasped, "y-yes, exactly like yours. You aren't her though, you look almost manly…I don't mean to offend you-"

"I've spent the totality of my being as a spectacle to the larger public, you cannot offend me." Niamé concluded their brief energy session, tears poured urgently down Citronella's cheeks.

"I've never felt a sensation like that"

"You have never allowed yourself to be open to the healing energies of an *other*. What you experienced just then, was a release of toxicity," Niamé assured.

Niamé bent closer to Citronella and opened the palm of their hands, a holographic distortion portrayed a sun lit laboratory. Rows of incubators encased with screaming babies filled the lab, as adults dressed in long white coats crowded over microscopes and test tubes. One doctor walked over to an incubator and injected the intra-venous solution with a carefully labeled syringe. Niamé paused the hologram and zoomed in on the syringe.

"Only a few of my kind survived this session. My biological parents were devout Medusozoans, so when our master teachers presented an opportunity to advance and restore our culture, they offered me as spiritual sacrifice-" green liquid shimmered from their left tear duct, "I could not choose my destiny, Citronella," Niamé quickly wiped the green film away and looked to the sky. For 100 eyeblinks, Niamé did not speak and instead focused their breathing. Citronella made several attempts during their stiff silence to unravel Niamé's emotions, which until then, seemed nonexistent.

"A truck is approaching, 30 miles North," Niamé abruptly informed Citronella, "the invisibility spell is using up too much of my energy, I need to rest…we will have to sneak on the truck, there I can probe the driver's mind and redirect us to our destination." Citronella was too tired to question Niamé's abilities. They waited for 20 minutes before the truck approached them; still invisible, they gently hopped onto the pickup truck and settled atop some sacks of manure.

"You've got to be kidding me, the only truck for miles and we had to lay on some shit?" Citronella tried to hold back her vomit.

"Be grateful, how can you be so spoiled when you've never had a pot to piss in?" Niamé humbled Citronella with their reasoning. It was not long before the truck driver noticed the two figures in the back and came to a rash stop, flinging them both into the back window shield. The driver quickly hopped out the truck and spoke to them angrily in Luganda: "Oyagala Ki nze? The man sucked his teeth.
"He's asking us what we want, I will tell him we are lost and ask for his help" Citronella, translated for Niamé.

"Osobola okumpitira yambakko ffe? Tubuzo" Citronella managed to conjure sincerity from her face and lowered her gaze. The older man sized her up and looked at Niamé who was barely clothed, with the exception of Citronella's work trousers and nodded at him.

"Nsonyiwa, nze Citronella," Citronella apologized for her ill manner.

"Ani oyo?" The man asked harshly, his eyes seemed to spit at Niamé.

"Boze Niamé, tasobola kutambula. Annina omusujja," Citronella placed her hand atop Niamé's forehead and sucked her teeth. The man seemed to lighten his tough stance and eased up to them.

"Ogenda wa?" He wants to know where we are headed, Citronella looked to Niamé.

"Kampala…"

"Sigenda Kampala" The man said surely and walked back to the truck door.

"Tell him we will compensate him his time," Niamé reasoned.

"But I do not have money, Niamé!"

"This, I consider to be a necessary time for root work," Niamé breathed deeply for some time, "go on and reason with him, I have something he may be interested in…"

"Ay! Ssente mmeka?"

"Olina ssente mmeka?" The man repetitively grazed his thumb against his index finger and showed the gaps of his teeth.

"Show him what you have," Citronella alluded the man's attention to Niamé. With an immediate force, Niamé grabbed a hold of the man's mouth and pried his jaws open. The man struggled to wrap his hands around Niamé's neck.

"What are you doing?" Citronella screamed.

"You'll see," Niamé reached inside of the man's mouth, until their hand was far into the esophagus. They toyed around in his throat and pulled out two small nuggets of gold.

"What the-" before Citronella could finish her obscenity, Niamé interrupted her, "ah ah ah! What did I tell you about your language, curse words were meant for just that, curses, be weary of your tongue, it may cause you a deal of trouble." Niamé released their left hand from the man's jaw, extended their right hand and waited for him to accept the gold. The man was stuck in silence until he coughed up some phlegm and spat it just past Niamé's feet. He grabbed the gold with a heavy hand and motioned them to get back into the truck, his face painted with a knowing fear. As they hopped atop the pickup truck, Citronella struggled to maintain eye contact with Niamé, unsure if she should fear him or be in awe.

"Excuse my abrasive force, it is hard to control once the root energy is ignited," Niamé offered a slow shrug.

The nameless man drove for quite some time; each pothole and bump in the road, reminded the triad of the humid night that held them in contempt. Citronella tried with great strength to hold onto the discharge that swam against the currents of her root, a blush waved over her face as she looked to Niamé.

"Is it Nostalgia again?" they asked earnestly.

"Yes, she usually waits to communicate with me when she senses I am alone…something must be up."

EXTENSION I

Descent
Into
Devolution

Post BodySnatcher was the age of MindFeeder. Where bodies were just an insulated projection of colors and numbers. A body's color emitted etheric auras, which made it prone to being read and thereby classified. Classification of color became synonymous to the essential perception of human body-ness; hues were determined by the mans and wombs in which they bodied.

In the year 2995, many native families along the Artic, Atlantic and Indian Oceans were fumigated from their homes; the rich and the poor were subjugated to a worldwide ethnic cleansing and branded with a number based on blood tests showing the numeric roots of their generational history. It didn't matter where a hue came from, or how ultra-violet their ray was, if their familial identification was greater than the number 9, they were sent to the Betamorphic processing camp. Every Betamorph was sanctioned into one of four, color auras; blue, green, yellow and purple. 99 problems and being a *minority* aint one.

I was only eleven when the Alphacorps first came to my country. They were gods to the children and elders alike. We were all awestruck at their strikingly confident features. They wore, what to us, looked like potato sacks, for them, it was the cloth of uniformity, "each stitch carefully woven by the headman of each household," a tribesman reported. They only wore the color black. They said blackness, was an affirmation of the melanated gods before us; how this black could be found in our atoms and in water just the same. Their skin as pale as the whites in every human's eye and as hard as the ice from which they came. My skin matched this black they praised so much. And yet it was I, who begged my mother and father for a pair of those blue eyes, went out of my way to dye my hair blonde; to be or not to be, that was the affliction.

The Alphas seemed to contest all sexual normalcies, we in each continent, had been conditioned to believe. The Alphacorp men were the cleaners, the cookers, the watchers of children, and the lovers; who seemed to spill milk from their very mouths. The women were cold with sunken chest, working and negotiating day and night with the elders of our community; silently studying us all they could and following us every chance we went to the mines (*clay edifices housing metals and minerals*). There was news of these people, who possessed little concrete evidence tracing them to one definite place, showing up unannounced at all sectors of the globe; trading nothing and asking for hospitality in return. It was change the Alphacorps preached, change in being, to rid humanity of outdated methods our mothers had been implementing for over two thousand years. They made us technologically dependent and gave God a new name.

They would come to our churches with their black books and preach the word of another God, this God still the divine trinity of heaven-human- earth, but more transcendent; able to manipulate space and time, sex and body, creed and origin, a worldly God,

a melanated God, whose blackness seemed to absorb
the shimmer of constellated stars. Those black books
in their hands we wanted so badly, to see if all of
what they said truly matched the ink on the page,
because if it was written, so it was...They wrote
nothing down, took no notes of our architectural
structures and left after twelve months of "cultural
immersion," it was only later that one of the
tribesman's known for thievery accused that black
book of having blank pages, how he threw such a
holy fragment to the wild rabbits. The Alphas
covered every piece of sand and spent one year on
each continent, after ten years they doubled back to
each place they ever visited and offered new
development blueprints. Out of all the continents, the
Alphacorp found it most favorable to settle along the
Gold Coast, a country in West Afriq. The last any of
us remembered seeing were masked armies of them
carrying automatic gas infusers, which put us all in a
deep sleep, as drones flew aimlessly over our heads
dropping iridescent nets to capture the runaways.

I remember a thick blanket of smog
covering every layer of the air, grabbing tightly to
every fixture, when I finally came to, I along with the
other children and elders were lying naked, covered
in bowel excrements; dried vomit blanketed my face.
Our bodies were not physically harmed as much as
our psyches, from seeing all of what we had built, all
of what was birthed from our mother's wombs and
our fathers hands, burn in flames, so easily. The
Alpha men, still sweet in their tongues would scream,
"One has to tear down in order to re-build! A place

must be ruined before it can be manicured! Just you wait...just you wait!" But we still cried and some of us even tried to fight those black- fearing Gods. It was then that everyone in my village banned the color black because the Alphas wore it so well with destruction. I suppose we never could find the god in melanin- not until now.

Scene 1

"3689!" four seconds later…

"I said 3689! One is calling you to the placebo portable and don't forget to bring your shit."
It was the thirty-second day of quitting spliffs and somehow there still seemed to be that benign lump in the core of my throat. The sensation was like spouting cotton, prickling drags of saliva, beading its way down with every third step toward Master One's corridor. The floor was made up of brown ice that created a muddy sleet with the warmth from my feet. Recently, the Alphacorp installed multiple silver lined refrigerant and water systems in all of their offices, for antibacterial purposes. Each room was like a walk in cooler, the exposed hairs on my skin ascended like tiny icicles. I could feel the dermis of my feet peeling with each step on the dry ice. We were near the equator and aside from the occasional bouts of rain, the sun shined with prominence, shoes were not a necessary commodity, when the earth of red soil provided a cushion for our soles. Only during the long walk to his office did I notice my ambivalence and regret for the culture. When I arrived, Master One was waiting under a cow bone lamp, it's light reflected yellow against One's peeled, blood orange skin. Master One sat there in silence, staring at the central computer system, watching.

"It took you long enough 3689."

"I'm sorry Master One, it was hard walking through the sleet, ya see, I have no sh-."

"Ah shut up, have you no concern for my precious time? Where is it?"

One liked to believe he was the ultimate being, but there was a higher power whose name was Aero, or Xero depending on the continent; she was hardly spoken of. Master One oversaw the Betas and spent most days monitoring all of the Auralites through a special edifice he called, "Placebo Portable." The Placebo Portable was very much like a University; young Betas are sent here for post-secondary learning and are assigned their fates, before carrying out their given function in the larger caste system.

"Here, sir, just as you wished, cover to cover of last night's proceedings."

"Very well then, need I remind you that this escapes your lips to no one, not even the rascals you call family. If this document and its whereabouts are placed in the wrong hands and spoken to the wrong ears, we can all suffer, myself included."

For the first time, I sensed a glint of fear on his brow and this made the knot in my throat tremble, I had forgotten the pool of blood at my bare feet and walked toward him.

"What do you think you're doing?" he reached back in his leather chair, fingers pressed to the cherry oak table. Although he preserved his guard, I could sense his heart, it's uneasiness, and I thought for a moment that I felt the same feeling in mine.

     Master One was the first Alphacorp executive to establish a core curriculum in the processing camp, that exceeded the approved learning curves of governing forces. One held bi-monthly lectures in his Placebo Portable. Topics ranged from apartheid to xenophobia. Lectures lasted four hours every Saturday Sabbath because all 53 students were eager to keep up the education that had been stripped from us at the end of our primaries. The beginning of each class was devoted to the Affirmation of Allegiance:

> *We, the purple Auralite Betas of Placebo Post-Secondary Learning, affirm our spirits and minds to the developed dedication of continued community bridging, through thought, word and action, any ideas spoken and subsequent actions pursued under the confinements of the PPSL Portable shall not be relieved to outside forces*

     Saturday after Saturday, these were the words drilled into our heads. Master One was always dotting his eyes and crossing his tees, everyone knew he was only an Alphacorp by blood and a Beta revolutionary by morale. Master One wasn't like those *Jim Crow Uncle Toms* (the paternalistic type, branding commonality with the traction of his leather boot on tar baby backs), he showed us from preserved Xerox copied history books of centuries long past. Though he was desensitized and his skin seemed to brown like that of a wound scabbing over, I could see layers in the crevice of his being. I occasionally thought to myself, perhaps with more careful probing, maybe one of his scars would resurface, unveiling the causality of his wrinkled ways.

Aero always kept tabs on Master One and sometimes made surprise sit-ins on his lectures. She would float in, sometimes appearing out of nowhere, the same silken blacks and greys draping her body. She seemed to be made of neatly compacted dust particles; hues of purple and black shimmered from her imaginary pores. Her eyes were hallowed out and she would cover them with mirrored sunglasses, she said, "the better to see your soul with." For anyone who tried to make eye contact with her, they could only see the fear on their own faces. Aero only feasted on the flesh of firstborns with physic *abnormalities*. At least 70 reports of child abductions are reported each year in the Gold Coast.

"What is he teaching you?" I heard her whisper to a student once, while uniting her index finger to the girl's forehead. Aero, rumored to have the touch of God or some devilish counterpart, made the young girl tremble. Ever since her encounter with Aero, 4778's eyes have been a glossy black; the sclera absent behind her enlarged pupils.

Speculation traversed that Master One, at some point, was just as gritty as Aero, maybe even worse. Before the takeover, One was just a scrawny yellow aura-light, his only saving grace being his family's subservient connection to a group of trillion-heirs. They gave him a conditional offer that only upon qualification, would advance his social standing. One had spent the bulk of his adolescence and adulthood training to be one of the most prestigious special agents; a MindFeeder.

The longing for a better life, made him cold, he worked tirelessly to mold himself into a caricature of their approval. Master One's sole task was to obliterate the minds of his own people, through a series of brainwashing and identity re-assignment sessions. I suppose the power trip couldn't last long before he lost his sanity… or gained a conscious. Something shifted within him after Aero ordered him to wipe out our last indixene race of the Gold Coast. One became more deviant and took on fewer operations. Aero noticed the unwavering change in Master One and kept closer tabs on his every move.

Aero inspected the notebooks of every student, even tore pages out, those she considered, "too imbedded with critical analyses of commoner-rebellion." She would always joke, "I'll have to start sleeping with my wand I see..." Everyone knew she didn't need a wand for some higher power, all she needed was imbedded in the locks of her hair; they would mop the floor if she did not keep them manicured in an up-righteous bun. She only wore her hair down whenever the Alphacorp law needed re-enforcement. Aero always threatened to put an end to the Placebo lectures... she never did. It seemed like they had a weird understanding, Aero gave Master One, unlike any other employees, complete autonomy. At times, a twinkle of envy washed over me whenever I saw them in seemingly intimate contact.

I knew Master One took to favoring me when he asked me after a lecture to assist him with *Operation Scheme*. Let him tell it, "Operation Scheme has been in effect long before my naming it." He said, "it arose translucent and collar-like, on the necks of the most vibrant of colors, how no one could ever see it, there was only this numbing effect on their minds." IIe was impressed at how I never took notes but seemed to be the most engaged, I told him, "notes were for the blind." Somehow my body was pulled back into the present, a sphere of tiny compacted energy gleamed just before my reach and disappeared as I became aware of Master One's hand waxing and waning over my eyes.

"You ever been under hypnosis?" Master One asked pointedly.

"Not to my knowledge," I chuckled nervously. Master One snapped his fingers three times and ran his right index finger from my pineal gland to my nose. "When the alarm goes off, you will fall under a deep paralysis, pay attention to my voice and any other sounds you may notice. Your sense of sight will be temporarily unavailable."

beep beep...beep beep...beep beep...beep beep...

A wave of familiarity washed over as a gust of wind blew forcefully in my ears. The sound of bells chiming brought a wave of nostalgia. In the distance, I could hear One reciting some weird algorithm, or molecular formula. A sweet smell of yams filled my nostrils. I breathed in deeply and allowed my stomach to expand and collapsed to my spine. I continued this deep breathing for some time, the warm feeling of an old southern comfort taught by my ancestors, was quickly replaced by a strong choking sensation. My breaths grew faint. I grappled with my native tongue and still no words came out, only the faint sound of my sub-conscious. One's tone grew louder and more urgent, this time yelling,

$$C_{18}H_{10}N_2O_4!... \quad C_{18}H_{10}N_2O_4!... \quad C_{18}H_{10}N_2O_4!...$$
$$C_{18}H_{10}N_2O_4!...$$

You must stop them from extracting the melanocytes! For a moment, my body floated through a darkened planal field. The same tingling sensation crept from my pineal gland to the base of my nose. My eyes were crusted over and took a while to adjust to the mustard light of his cow bone lamp.

"How do you feel?"

"What was the point of that?" I asked him in earnest confusion.

"It would have been less effective to have a simple conversation with you about Operation Scheme, Kalic, but that was not enough to make you feel the urgency of this assignment." Master One circled his eyes around the dim room and locked in on an anatomy book, "I suppose the term hypnosis, diminishes the authenticity of this exchange," he looked around once more before continuing his idea.

"What I just did, bound us indefinitely through psychical and physical terms. Every time you hear that alarm, it will be a message from me." Master One appeared to have more on his mind but settled into his ergonomic hover chair.

"Couldn't you just use our innate mind tracking system to communicate inaudibly with me?"

"Yes, I could have, but our minds are connected to the larger Alphacorp systems network. Any official with standing authority, at will, can initiate mental access and gather data. It is safer to communicate this way."

"So, this is kind of like a firewall?"

"It gives us private user access, bound by a spell, inaccessible to third parties…"

"Can I use this firewall to communicate with you before you contact me?"

"I'm glad you asked this, it's quite tricky, but I am confident in your ability to pick things up quickly…while you were under hypnosis, there were certain images and smells you witnessed, do you remember the order?"

"Umm, I think," I stared into the burning gaze of the orange lamp and waited for the memories.

"I heard the bells chime, then a sweet smell like candied yams, I deep breathed for some time and then you yelled the molecular formula for melanin."

"You are missing a few details," One waited impatiently, "think, don't blurt the first things you remember, try again."

"Gee, where'd your confidence go?"

Master One chuckled and then said with fervency, "into an abyss, recite!" Kalic tapped into his subconscious and closed his eyes, blocking every distraction of the physical realm, a brief wind settled atop his exposed skin, giving him goosebumps. "I heard the bells; your voice was muffled in the background and I tried to make it out but couldn't. The sweet smell of yams swept under my nose…I started breathing in, opening my stomach and exhaling everything from within me," Kalic stopped and grabbed his neck before continuing, "then a choking sensation came over me and I could not speak! All of a sudden you were yelling the formula for melanin, repetitively," Kalic opened his eyes and looked at Master One. Without moving his lips, One spoke to Kalic, "very well, young one, do you think you can remember that combination?"

"I'll try my hardest! -"

"You'll have to do more than try! Pay attention to your senses, you can miss out on a great deal of trouble if you listen to yourself. Remember that if nothing else..."

"So, what does $C_{18}H_{10}N_2O_4$ have to do with Operation Scheme?"

"The Alphas have been slowly performing cosmetic enhancement surgeries on the lower class population. They've been extracting pineal glands, which naturally produce melatonin and melanocytes that generate our dark pigmentation," Master One caressed his blackened orange skin. "They are experimenting with people like you, you're disposable in their eyes, Kalic...after extraction, they then replace the pineal with a third-dreyeve."

"What's that?"

"A secondary optical and psychical unit that transcribes external information and is then stored into their larger operating system."

"Why are they doing this?

"Is this actually a shock to you? We are literally in a test tube, being spied on!" Master One broke psychical communication and gave me orders to wait for further correspondence on the assignment, then motioned me out of his office.

Scene 2

"We've been on this floor long enough, there might be gravel in the crack of my-"

"Va, stop your bitching, they are almost done and tone it down, this is a stakeout, not an open mic"

"What the fuck are we even doing here, Kalic? It's cold as shit and we've missed the last block for dinner, I'm starv"-

"You are making me internally scream right now, good lord, you could've stayed home, now you're here ruining all chances of us not being found out! I'm clocking the time these Alpha- fucks make their rounds."

Something about the cold gravel and feelings of quasi-mysticism made my root hard. It was like waking up bare bodied in a flannel sleeping bag, tent surrounded by grey woods with cardinals staring viciously, as if they knew the seeds that were planted the night before. I grew up with Va on the Southern gulf of Ghana, we frequented Mo' Body Beach and when the tides were mellow, we took baths in the ocean together. We created our own monthly rituals, called sea cleanses. We snuck out half past midnight, when our elders were asleep and bathed in silence. The ocean had enough stories to tell us; we listened. We dove naked, head first and let the cool thrash of the waves swallow us whole, let them crash against our surrendered bodies and never cursed the wounds that followed. Perhaps these ceremonies were just an excuse to dive naked with one another, catch glimpses of authenticity, unlike the conditioned reality the Alphas created for us. We would let our bodies sway involuntarily into the indigo nights' horizon. After we got carried away too far, our flailing arms would shovel back to the grains of sand made of our clothes.

On our fourth cleansing ceremony, the waves were unusually temperamental, my body submitted to each pull and I almost drowned. It seemed like I gulped gallons of salt water. I kept reaching for pastel purples and sparkles of magenta light with weighted palms, spheres of air escaped my vessel. Va, fortunately, was a long distance swimmer and never inhaled petro like the rest of us who were starving to escape this reality. Va saved me, she always does. She dragged me back to shore, the needy fog added an extra layer of skin to us. It was then that I decided to show her the scars on my back. She took her hands and covered me with the reddish sand from toe to head; that was the second time her lips ever touched mine. She said she watched her mother work her fingers at the root of her father and how she saw another light, which came from his diaphragm. She tried this on me, she thought this would soothe me. It made me remember the time our mouths were full of imported cookies, sweet and foreign kisses.

Va was there the night I ran over to her compound, blood swimming from my pants, with the same salt water veiling my eyes. She held me and I rocked back and forth in her arms, whispering all the things that devil had done to me; how he managed to open me. She knew when it started and knew that it never ended until the Alphacorps captured us. Some part of me was relieved at the separation from my foster parents, the other part of me missed his filling, and I remained open. Va knew this and tried her hardest to touch me with the hands only a mother could manage, the same hands her mother and her mother's mother, and her mother's mother's mother, and all the mothers before would use to touch their seeds; enduring their growth.

There were many young men like me, shattered with the comfort of a male presence, finding security in the way someone could weed at our roots of manhood; how this presence was unapologetic and made me and the rest of the cowardice boys yield under its seizure. Va knew how fond I was of Master One and so any chance she could, she would always be there with us. I could not tell her just yet, of our private meetings. Almost completely out of my daze, I heard a footsteps cringe at the right of where we were stationed; hidden between the barracks beside the heaps of plastic crates, filled with recycled sack-uniforms.

"Yo 1497! Where do ya keep these tapes?"

"Anh, inside that file cabinet next to the water barrels"

"Ay'd you see that purple glow from over by the uniform dispensary? I tried to lock in on the aura field but there was too much static between our range and the plastic crates"

"Na, I'll go check it out though"

"Ay Va! I think they're headed over here, lets shift to the main entry"

"17:30," I whispered into my audible wristband.

"Fuck this Kalic, if I get into any more shit, I'll have two orders on me and I'm not-"

"Shut up, just stick behind me."

We were weaving through the crates; odors of sweaty balls and butts filled our noses. The barracks were right along the old dock where all the Beta ship breakers (*teenaged street kids and young adults were the ones to work this sight because no person over the age of thirty would even think of laboring for the Beta ship breaker dock, let alone be satisfied with the shitty pay*) were stationed.

To buy us more time, I focused my breathing on stabilizing my invisibility cloak chakra and wrapped my arms around Va's naval and pineal openings. I learned this technique from the confidential documents Master One desperately wanted me to keep a secret. This document housed well over 360 karmic spells and commandments used by Aero and her nine disciples. Before handing the document over to Master One, I scanned a copy to my Retinal Intuit Processor. Somehow during the Alpha takeover, there was a glitch in the system and a few Betamorphs, like myself, were able to retain our photographic memories. So far, I have memorized 118 spells; only those I felt could serve me during this time of Beta Revolution.

After veiling our auras with the invisibility cloak chakra, officer 1497 walked right through us, before Va could yelp in shock, I kissed her and held my lips to hers until the officer was more than fifty feet away from us. She looked at me quizzically.

"I'll tell you all about it later," I promised and thrusted her body forward with mine. We were just at the main entry gate when the officer, whose numeric ID I failed to make out, jolted at my left ankle with some weird spiked metal; each prong teethed to the nerves of my ankle skin, causing me to slip. I yelled for Va, "Keep running, I'll meet you at our spot! Go!"

The chubby officer dived for my idle body and I faked him with a turn-over, I pulled the spiked arch out of my ankle and bashed his head in with my good foot. Officer 1497 was approaching much faster then I calculated. I had just enough time to initiate the tri-eye laser chakra I practiced the night before, but because I did not fully master it, I was only able to put him in a standing comatose position, that would wear off in about sixty seconds. Just to be safe, I pressure pointed the unknown officer's larynx and grabbed the security camera on the front of his chest. I ran for the gate, wheezing, I took a drag from my crystalized albuterol and continued weaving through the Beta-ship-breakers intersections until I finally arrived at the chemical pond.

The chemical pond was the only body of water Va and I found, to replace the ocean that was once our haven. Although we knew it to be the water enemy, we spent hours there, pouring prayer into being. She was there sitting with the same quizzical look on her face she had left me with back in the barracks.

"What the hell is going on Kalic? We could've died back there!"

"Yeah, well we didn't," I tried to say nonchalantly.

"Yeah, well how in the world did you manage superpowers back there" she asked me in an equally matched satirical tone.

"Va, there are some things I just can't disclose to you yet!"

"Who do you th-"

"Listen, it's all related to Operation Scheme, and that's as much as I'm telling you for now, once I meet with Master One, I'll know for sure."

"So, One's behind this shit? I knew you two were up to something Kalic, just..."

"...Be safe, I know Va," she looked at me with those mothering eyes and suggested that we go back to her compound and change clothes.

Scene 3

Every Betamorph was piled in little Victorian style edifices in the middle of the Betamorph Processing camp, while all the Alphacorps were assembled on the outskirts of the camp, to ensure the preservation of our enslavement. Va lived in Compound 87, I lived only eleven doors up from her. Since we used the public air transit, it took us only twenty-two seconds to get home. Once we got to her compound, she pulled out some of her brother's clothing for me, I quickly changed. We both thought it best that I cut and dye the hair I'd been growing for nine years, to avoid being identified. I told Va I needed some of what the haa-my-kin Betamorphs called "chronic" before I could go through with such an emotionally draining ID process, so we scraped up some loose copper [1]wires and she hovered up to compound 420 for some of that *chronic*.

When Va got back she had a spooky look on her face, "turn on the news Kalic, hurry!" I grabbed the general compound controller and pressed the "TV" button, once the monitor was on, there was a collage of 12 different channels showing the same blurry clip of two purple Auralites; a young woman whose face barely missed the cop's camera, and a young man hunched on the ground with his face down, the only thing traceable was the tattoo on his left ankle.

---

[1] Natural stones and metals were the currency.

"Oh shit," I looked in amazement at Va.

"Valerian, this could be the end."

"No, no, they didn't zone in on our faces Kalic, we could be anyone! But one things for sure, we gotta get that tattoo of yours covered, like now!" She said with a desperate look.

"Well did you at least grab the *chronic*," I asked her.

"Yea, affirmative," she threw me the bag and headed to the kitchen to grab a knife, some ammonia, hydrogen peroxide, aloe vera and her grandfather's old blowtorch. I grabbed the flask from my right thigh pocket and took a long hard swig of the vintage moonshine one of my coworkers had gifted me for my 21st solar return, a few weeks back. Va slowly walked over to me with the utensils in her hand and a twisted grin on her face, like she had been waiting for this moment her entire life, to be the one to cause my pain.

"Whose bitching now!?" She said sarcastically. She tied me down to her bed; my hands cuffed with belts to her headboard and my legs triple wrapped in rope, enough to show my ankle tattoo. We figured the best way for me to ingest the chronic was through the air ventilating machine her grandmother had to use nightly for her congested lungs. Va filled the mask capsule with grinded chronic particles and flipped the machine switch on as she placed the mask over my mouth and nose. Gas hurriedly filled the room and she began her procedure *once my eyes were a shade of blood burgundy.*

On my ankle, were two Koi fishes, both swimming in opposite directions, to capture my dualistic journey as a Gemini. Va would always argue that it was more of an ode to the Piscean sign and so I was sure she loved this moment of finally being able to get rid of my, "mark of contradiction," as she called it.

Va took the knife and scraped at my skin, I tried hard to clench back my screams but when she poured the ammonia on my wound I couldn't resist, "GAHHH!" She punched me in the face before I could finish such a deadly yelp and I passed out. When I woke up, I was still on her bed, but untied. She had opened all the windows to clear the smoke before her family got back from their field shifts and watched me with a yeast beer in her hand.

"Go check it out chump," she said as I wiped the sweat from my brow and bounced to her closet door mirror.

"Eck," I felt a piece of vomit trying to swim up my throat, but I swallowed the little guy back down and continued to frown at my ankle's reflection in the mirror.

"It looks like I got gnawed by a pool of fire breathing dragons! What if they start a random search and see this mark, don't you think they'll be suspicious, Valerian?" I preached to her.

"Maybe, but we can always come up with some galactic excuse, something health- related! She threw me a neat pack of crushed ice and told me to apply it directly to the wound for one week, around the clock. I left her compound and hobbled back to mine, seeing double, descending from my chronic-state. When I opened the door, Master One was sitting on my XenoBoy trill-thousand recliner.

"What is this blasphemy, 3689!?" He spat at me while projecting the news clip from his eye-ban solar-glasses.

"I can spot that ugly tattoo you sport around from a mile away!" He jumped up and grabbed me by the arm, pushing me into the trill-thousand, studying my newfound wound.

"Ahh, you're not as dumb as I thought you were... I guess..."

"Well, now there'll be a questionable scar on my-"

"Don't worry about the scar, I've got just the medicine to heal that, in a few hours it will look like it's never existed," he chuckled to himself.

"Wait here," he said.

Five minutes later, he reappeared at my door, this time knocking considerately, making up for his last intrusion.

"Whelp, here you go," he handed me some foul smelling ointment (*crushed cranberries, cat-piss, fermented rose and aloe vera*).

"You think it smells bad, ha! Try consuming it twice a day for a week straight…topical application is nothing!"

I sat down on the trill thousand and he kneeled at my feet, took my left ankle by the hand and started massaging the ointment on my wound. The pleasure I felt exceeded the pain. I tried hard to train my mind on some ugly thing to keep my erection down. It didn't work. I knew he noticed, but he ignored it verbally, and with a slight smile he began drilling me for information.

"What time did the evening officers' shift start? What were they doing? How many of them were there? Why'd you bring Va? Does she know anything about Operation Scheme? Where are they hiding the files?"

He would've kept going if I hadn't held my palm to his mouth. He quickly removed my hand. "Well are you going to answer me!?"

"There are three bronze safes; Safe (*Sc*), Safe (*He*), and Safe (*Me*)…your presumptions were correct about Operation Scheme," I muttered.

"Well, did you use your optical scanner, what was inside?" One probed.

"They were all filled with files, video documentation and external hard-drives"

"And where are they located?" One asked annoyingly.

"Along the water barrels in the Beta-ship-breaker work site near the soiled uniforms. The security was pretty minimal during the shift change window from 17:26 hours to 17:32 hours. I'm unsure if the same officers work every night but we can totally get pass them-"

"We?" One encouraged. "You won't be anywhere near the sight again, tell me the IDs of each officer, so I can run a scan on them."

"1497...I didn't get the fourth digit of the second, 138- something- b-but, why can't I..."

"What good are you if you can't remember a basic sequence with your retinal processor? My god 3689, maybe this was too much of a task for a boy," he looked down at my now less erect root in disgust.

"Forgive me, Master One, an officer clipped my ankle with some metal razor! But I used the tri-eye chakra to hold him off for a whi-"

"You did what!?" He slapped his hand against his forehead, "I should've known you would download the documents to your inner drive," he stood over me, now erect in posture and lifted me by the neck. My laryngeal prominence scraped the palm of his grip, he felt this, and squeezed harder. "Listen, Kalic, I won't have you ruin this for me, what all do you know?" The trail of his "know" hit my nostrils with a moist and probing air.

"I...cant..." he let go of my neck and I fell helplessly back into the chair, "...breathe."

"I want you to hold onto that question, you're coming with me." He grabbed a hold of my pineal and once I re-opened my eyes, we were standing in the middle of what seemed to be the prisoner-processing pipeline. There were consecutive rows of huge capsulated water tanks, idle bodies floated, a weird umbilical cord connected the tops and bottoms of each tank. One said it wasn't water that was sustaining their weakness, but what the Alphas called, "Cola-Krypton," a chemical extract from the late-crazed 1900s, crack-cocaine, and *War On Drugs* bust. Master One said that exposure of this newly enhanced drug to the Beta-psyche, would surely emit them into an abyss, "and if you keep screwing up, I'll see to it that you end up here," he threatened.

As we strolled down the aisles of capsulated tanks, Master One used his skin-sensory thumb drive to gather all the karmic spells and commandments from my retinal intuit processer. A green Auralite cop came in for his routine round, Master One quickly removed his thumb from my third eye. The immediate cease of force made my body tremble.

"What we got here, Master One," Officer 1385 chuckled at us. The pool around my feet started weighing me to the surface as I studied the scar on his face.

"Oh nothing, Jack, One didn't bother checking the officer's badge, "just some dumb delinquent who was bad mouthing me in class last Sabbath, I wanted to show the sucker where he could end up," Master One scowled at me as I began to dance in place.

"Y'know kid, maybe my eyes must be getting old, but you look mighty familiar, haven't I seen you somewhere? After that beating yesterday, my brains been a little skewed," 1385 stated questioningly and towered over the young man. Master One intervened before I could manage a response, "Officer, this kid is trouble but he's not foolish, besides he was with me after office hours, compiling some literature for my next lecture."

"Careful One, you can't trust youth these days with a one foot pole! Y'see what one of the snatchers did to my face," Officer 1385 said unveiling the gauze around his forehead.

"I'm surprised you're still working, 1385, with a laceration like that, you should be accumulating energy for optimal recovery," Master One suggested. Officer 1385 now with his back to us, continued on with his rounds, "you may be right Master One but I know the sucker is coming back, I want to be here when he does…sweet day Auralites, I have to keep on the watch," he shouted into the blackness of the dim-lit pipeline room.

"That was him Master One, that was the other officer," anxiety spewed from my whispers.

"Are you sure?" Master One knew I was sure but asked again anyway, "Are you sure he's the other officer?" I nodded my head as he dragged me to the exit, "we have to strategize, we have to strategize," he mumbled.

"Oh, its 'we' now eh?" I said satirically.

Scene 4

It was   2567 eye-
blinks

after the mass marketed news coverage of the green
Auralite assault down at the ship-breakers dock.
There were swarms of Alphacorp officials and aura-
nosing Betamorphs trailing the entire town for leads
and eyewitnesses or gossip jugglers of the crime. No
one could divulge useful information. Master One
departed from me in contemplative haste, forgetting
to erase the karmic lessons from my hard drive. We
reconvened that night, 2100 sharp, on the side alley
of my compound complex.

"We need to act fast," Master One said. "You know
where the rest of the files are, right? Let's retrieve
them."

"Are you positive you want to risk potentially being
caught? Imprisoned? Exiled?" I pleaded in question
to him.

"There is no right time Kalic, then the time ticking,
justice is always plotting."

I reached for his pineal to begin the teleportation
process but Master One apprehended from the
potentiality of my touch.

"Do not get ahead of yourself, 3689, I will lead the
way…besides when we arrive, you will need all your

energy to perform the necessary karmic affirmations," he winked.

We landed near the far left end of the ship-breaker work site. The crates of recycled uniforms I mapped for recall, were transferred to the dock's outskirts, so it would be a feat getting past the green auralite officials. "They moved the files," I whispered to Master One.

"Then we must use our optical scanners to zone in on the paper trail," he assured me.

Master One cultivated enough energy from the air and breathed himself into invisibility and began snooping around the border's premises; I followed him. As much as we could hide our physical selves, we could not mute our sounds. My right foot met the gravel abruptly and sent a ripple into the ears of one of the watch-robots. "Seriously?" Master One gave me an annoyed expression.

"Alert, green Auralites, there is an aura tremor vibrating from field zone seven," the watch-robot reported.

"Copy, Officer 1874 on alert and in motion."

Officer 1874 reached into her back left pocket and re-surfaced a tiny silver ball; she pressed into the center of it, transforming her entire left arm into a magnified projector, in which she was able to get a close-up image profile on all the objects she hovered. With each stroke of her arm in front of an object, the projector ticked in metronome, "tack tack tack…" as she scanned in all directions, her projectile meter hastened once it reached our direction. "Looks like we got something here…" she mumbled to herself, the watch-robot hovering at her right.

As the two officials neared, Master One broke his invisibility cloak and managed to keep me veiled, I quickly used my optical scanner to trace down the bronze safes and crept toward the far south of the work site, away from the officers.

"Master One, what are you doing in the Beta-breaker-site? We didn't see your id tag on the entrance scanner…"

"Report your number when addressing me, officer"

"I apologize sir, I'm Officer 1874…all of the control units have been on strict watch due to the purple on green Auralite assault that took place here last night…"

Master One walked over to the officer and sized her from root to crown, "I am here for the exact same reason you are, 1874, to extract clues for yester-night's happenings…do I need authorization?" One asked sarcastically.

"Uh, uh, no sir, not at all…your energy just threw me off and my projector did not pick up on your ID…"

"Here is some advice 1874, on each watch, make sure your internal hard-drive is updated…and next time…avoid questioning me."

"Noted, Master One. Please forgive my querying, Officer 1385 and I will continue scanning the ship site for DNA and evidence."

"Did you say, Officer… 1385? That guy never stops," Master One chuckled, "Well, I'll continue my private investigation now," his stare left the officer stiff in solitude.

"Do call out to us-" Officer 1874 struggled to say as Master One evaporated into the ethers, "-if you find anything."

Master One teleported near the direction of irregular Beta-beats (*heartbeats*), he was sure belonged to Kalic. "What good is your invisibility cloak if I can hear your Beta-beats 100 klicks away?" Kalic was desperately stabbing away at the bronze enamel of the safe. Both Kalic and Master One were unaware that Officer 1385 and 1874 were lurking behind some of the soiled uniform crates using secondary canal-drum devices to interpret their every word.

"Aero is a lot smarter than you think young man, shem would not make the safe malleable to any karmic affirmations that can be projected by a mere Beta, you see that sheath of black glass below the punch code?" And without a response Master One continued to answer his question, "that is the *latest* optical scanning device, access is required from select pupils."

"I assume Aero is among the select pupil?"

"Your assumption is correct Kalic; Aero and the crafts-kin of these safes. There was speculation that she killed the manufacturers to avoid any tamper with these documents...you scraping at them with metal won't do a damn thing."

"So, we need her eyes," Kalic fumbled resolutely.

"Let's get you out of here, Officer 1385 is on rounds again and your invisibility cloak is nearing its end." Master One swept Kalic's feeble body under his arm and vanished into a small spectrum of orange light.

"Those dim-witted coms!" Officer 1385 whispered to Officer 1874, "wait until Aero hears this feed." Officer 1874 turned her canal-drum device off before replying and gestured for him to do the same. Officer 1385 fumbled to disarm his body camera before incriminating himself.

"Are you sure we should take it to her so soon? I mean, what if they can lead us to some information we've been-" Officer 1874 attempted to reason.

"You're right," 1385 speculated.

"We've been runnin' around like automated zombies for Aero, with nothing to show for it but a green aura-field. I was better off being a purple Beta, at least I could look at myself in the mirror," Officer 1874 looked to the 1385 and bowed her head.

"Listen, 1874, we could've took the spiritually conscious role, but we did this to put food on our table and live comfortably," Officer 1385 gave her a hard pat on the shoulder before continuing, "we have to keep our enemies as close as possible, Aero's planning something huge and we want every player out of the way."

"So, you would sacrifice Master One, your only lead," Officer 1874's words stung.

"That boy is his disciple, there's no telling how many other Betas he's indoctrinated, did you see that scar on his left ankle?" 1385 picked at his unmanicured beard, the perp that got away yesterday had a tattoo on his left ankle.

"That's not too much of a lead, 1385, let's just keep this information for backup, we need to know the contents of those safes," Officer 1874 schemed.

"And what do you think will happen to us if Aero finds out we knew they were plotting something before we mentioned it to her? Do you think we'll get some badge of honor, a pat on the back? We've got to stay ahead of this," Officer 1385 stalled on his words. 1874 shifted in her stance and looked to the soiled uniforms.

"Just hold off for a while, I've got an idea."

Scene 5

The sun was rising now and peach hues were battling the contempt of indigo's night. There was something unsettling in how the fog raptured the sky. "Kalic's been gone for some time now," Va thought to herself while she prepared hot water for her elders' bath. Va's grandmother was the keeper of their families traditional recipes. She stood with the wizened slump of a sage at the kitchen counter. She had already prepared pounded yam porridge, "you will learn one day baby, that certain memories will never escape your hands, even after years of ethnic cleansing," she cautioned her grand-daughter, "it took us eons to learn and its taking them centuries to destroy," queen mother smiled at Va, surety in her eyes.

90 blinks were the equivalent of years as Va waited for Kalic's update

It was a regular work day for her household, when Va was not in Master One's Sabbath class, she was teaching her own in urban gardening. Va was riding the Beta southbound public air train to the community garden, when a nearby air train from the oncoming northern direction exploded, sending bus debris and shrapnel in fleeting directions. The southbound bus tipped over due to the combustive impact and descended for a few hundred feet before the pilot could steady the wheel; unfortunately, it was too late, the bus crashed to the pavement and rolled a few times before settling into complete destruction.

It took only 123 eye-blinks before officials and health teams were on site and only one person's wrist cam to make the act of terror go viral. 18 deep breaths later when Va came to, the bus was still on its side and the air was a charcoal grey. Her ears were ringing but she made out the sounds of a rescue team. Voices trailed in and out of her immediate hearing.

The rescue team used multiple laser cutters to make five large circular slices through the metal, since the bus had fell on the right side where the doors were stationed. Adults and children were moaning in pain as the stench of seared skins pervaded their senses. Va's eyes started fluttering, revealing only the sclera and later alerted by a stinging yank. Now conscious, she realized that half of her body was being thrusted through shards of the jagged metal opening.

"Ma'am, ma'am, please respond if you can hear me   (*pause*)   you and the others are being taken to the Beta Clinic for treatment   (*pause*) you've been severely wounded," a friendly nurse coached her, "please take a deep breath so I can check your vitals". It took three Beta-medics (*paraprofessionals*) to lift Va from the slumbering bus, her bloodied hands clutched her messenger bag with a strenuous force.

Valerian was placed onto the stretcher and into an ambulance where she grew hostile as they kept probing her tender skin with needles. Two Beta-medics worked eagerly to remove her scarlet soiled articles and replaced them with a one size fits all hospital gown.

"This may hurt," the nicer Beta-medic warned as she covered Va's wounds with a damp gauze of alcohol. Va squirmed and pulled the Beta-medic by the collar.

"Wh-But whe- where's my phone, I need my phone!" forgetting the pain, Va jerked up from the stretcher, "I need my fucking phone!" In less than two eye blinks she had already removed the last needle connected to her intravenous solution.

"Ma'am, Miss Valerian, we have it here, as well as the rest of your belongings, some of it is a bit scratched up and bloodied because you were holding them so tightly, even while unconscious," one of the Beta-medics assured her.

"Where is it?" Va demanded, cold sweat and smoky dust tinting her face. "Here, it's right here," the same Beta-medic handed Va her phone and messenger bag. Unbothered by her current state, Va dodged pass the Beta-medics and kicked open the ambulance door, stumbling onto the hilly pavement.

Perhaps it was the hybrid dosage of amphetamines and sedatives, or Valerian's obsession to find Kalic that had her nonchalantly walk bare assed in the streets. She staggered for what seemed to be two miles, constantly looking down at the raw meat made of her skin, until she came across a convenient store.

She pushed the door in forcefully and left behind a smear of maroon on the glass.

"Lady, what happened to you? Where are your clothes?" a young woman behind the counter turned her mouth up in dismay and called for someone to the front, "yo Q! I need some assistance, this woman's leaking all over the place!"

"I was in an accident, t-t-the train plummeted a-a-and," Va began to tremble in shock. The young woman behind the counter looked at the television monitor and turned to Va, "Oh snap! The news reporters are saying the air bus explosions are some sort of terrorist attack! I'm glad you're alive ma'am, but you don't look good...Q! Get out here!"

"What is it, Nova, I'm on bre-" The somewhat older looking man stared at Va, "you need to get to a hospital, miss." Valerian noticed something strange about these two Auralites, their colors seemed to change like thermochromic mood rings.

"I don't trust these medical officials, I just need some antiseptic and bandages, can you all help me?" Va leant onto the counter and sighed heavily.

Just outside, adults and children screamed in chorus to the melody of sirens. Kalic's text note appeared on her phone screen as if God shemself orchestrated the entire scene:

07:53

> Va, keep yourself and family home for a few
> days
> 07:54
> that's all I can say right now
> 08:11
> don't worry

It was too late, Va was already worrying and
nervously chewed the scraped skin that was left on
her knuckles. Nova closed down the shop and bolted
the metal accordion gate with three u-locks. Nova
disappeared from and returned with a sweat resistant
suit. Q walked Va to the back of the store. "Get
dressed," he pointed to the corner where a utility sink
was stationed. Q left the room and in eyeblinks
returned with a large first aid kit and a pint of rum.

"I know it don't look like it, but I come from healers,
I'll throw some sutures on a few of these but this one
is major," Q pointed to the large gash on Va's right
hip.

"Those fu- ahhh! So-called Beta-medics-" Va's
temper carried her away for a moment. "Well you
didn't give them much of a chance to help you,
miss!"

"I don't like getting the Alpha-government involved,
just leads to more bills and my name in more of their
systems."

"Relax, what's your name?"

"Valerian"

"Well Valerian, you're in good hands, now…take a swig of this here," Q passed her the bottle and waited for her cooperation. Va swung a generous mouthful to the back of her throat, the burn to her stomach felt like a massage compared to the abrasions on her body. After a few more shots she was knocked out, cold. A gentle nudge woke her up a few hours later.

"You're all set Valerian," Q grinned and walked back to the front of the store, closing the door behind him. Va took a few moments to sit up, the pain crept up on her like a sneak blow to the head and she fell back to the broken in leather couch. Nova appeared before Va's eyes out of nowhere, with a piping hot copper bowl.

"This will ease the tension in your muscles and joints," Nova ushered the spoon into Va's mouth.

"Ack! What did you put in here?"

"A few teaspoons of apple cider vinegar, black molasses, garlic and ginger. Your wounds are too fresh to be dressed in clove oil, so I'm running the oil diffuser…just sit here and breathe it in." Hours passed but the lingering need to find Kalic remained. She checked her real time navigation tracker for Kalic's whereabouts. His tracker pinned him near the bombing areas. Va quickly guzzled the soup down and grabbed her belongings, unbothered with

checking their contents. She hobbled out the
maintenance closet.

"Leaving so soon," Q caught Va's attention, "Nova,
was just about to bring you an herbal tea supplement.
You should really take some time to rest and
rehabilitate."

"Both of you have been a life saver, I truly don't
know how to repay y'all," Va snapped back into
reality and offered authenticity with warm eyes.

"You can start by never again showing up at our store
dripping in blood," Q chuckled, iron in his laugh, "all
jokes aside, be careful out there…if you ever need a
place to lay low, we have an underground unit for
safe keeping." Nova walked over to Valerian and
offered her wrist for a scan exchange, "we've got kin
all over this planet, don't hesitate," she swept a lock
of Va's hair from her face and proceeded to stuff her
hands with an air tight container of medicine.

"Take these with a full glass of water every three
hours for five consecutive days. It seems like you'll
be doing a lot of travelling, so remember to stay
hydrated and eat during or after each dosage," Nova
looked at Q before handing Valerian a backpack full
of dried goods and toiletries, "your turn." Q reached
out to Va, wrist first and waited for their internal
systems to synch, "we're all officially tapped in, now,
stay safe queen!"

"I appreciate you two more than you all know. Im
sure we'll meet again, blessings," Va slowly cringed

to the door and before leaving, looked back at the two, the couple resembled the perfection of melanated love she hoped to exude with Kalic.

Valerian started jogging South toward the green dot on her phone and found herself in the back alley of an eatery chain. Once she was in close proximity to Kalic, she stopped to catch her breath. There were rows of compost and recycle bins, Va was able to taste the aroma of brown sugar, bread and spoiled food; the stench made her queasy and she hunched over for a few minutes to muster some equilibrium. She finagled herself to see Kalic's body, she was standing meters away from the green dot.

"Kalic!"   (*Pause*)
"Hey Kalic   (*Pause*)
                    you there?"
She opted to call him to avoid drawing any attention. His phone rang and she followed the chirping sound. The phone was lying underneath a shallow board of wood with a note taped to the back:

> *I figured you would keep tabs, Valerian, so I had to get rid of my phone. I've gotten myself in some deep shit following after him. You can't risk your physical safety for my decisions. Please don't try to find me, I will be alright. What happened earlier was only a distraction but know that you must protect yourself and family. Move, now! This country isn't safe and Im afraid we've only made matters worse.*

*I love you Va, I never got to tell you that
evening at the Beta ship breakers site, but
that kiss was real. You've been patient with
me, know that I want more than anything, to
share more time with you. Be well Va,
Yours Forever,*

Kalic

Valerian held back the tears and trudged
angrily toward an air train station headed in the
direction of the Placebo Portable. She was sure Kalic
would be with Master One. Nausea swept her into the
unknown. The attackers managed to hit each transit
route within the district; consequently, there were re-
directive signs sanctioned by each transit entrance,
which significantly delayed her travel time. Va
decided to walk on foot, amidst the other frazzled
Auralites, colors swirled around rapidly in reaction to
everyone's emotive state. It took her a few hours to
get to the Placebo Portable. Sweat moistened her
wounds but the pain was not enough to keep her from
knowing the truth.

Master One's Placebo Portable was just an
extension of the larger Alphacorp Head Quarters. His
office was unlike the typical phallic institution style
building; it was in ovular shape, the glass ceilings
captured sunlight justly. Valerian strategized on how
to slip past the security officers and climb to the roof
of his workspace. Fortunately, the sun was beginning
to settle, which made her less conspicuous. Va
crouched for what seemed like an eternity, until a

crew worker appeared on a mini cart. *Divine timing.* Va hopped onto the back caddy and waited until she found a clear opening to One's office.

Scene 6

Master One was back in his office typing furiously under his cow bone lamp when Aero appeared in his doorway. He stretched his hand into the top right drawer for the sacred wood and lighter.

"What brings you to my office," One asked Aero, while he placed the objects in his pants pocket. She circled around his desk and removed her mirrored glasses revealing the death in her eyes. "You seem to be where all the trouble is, One."

"I'm not sure what you are referring to…" Master One searched through her black-holes, the lie seeming to be sucked from his brow.

"You fail to remember…No, you seem to have ignored the omniscience of my being. I am everywhere One…even in your thoughts." Aero reached toward Master One's mandibular region and cracked it with one motion, "since you cannot speak truth, you mustn't speak at all," sharp edges of bone protruded from his jaw.

"You see, it took quite a while before I was made aware of your *scheme*. It's sad, even the boy has no idea of your culture, your gifts, your true name!…but leave it to some eager green Auralites, anxious to climb the Alpha ladder," Aero chuckled and intercepted the canal drum device of the officers lurking just beyond the eye. She squatted a few inches from One and picked up his slacked jaw.

"So, you're not that omniscient, eh Aero," Master One looked up at her haphazardly. He struggled to form another sarcastic remark but Aero removed the support of her hand from his mouth.

"My higher self was telling me to stave you off, years prior. You're right, my knowledge of your operation did not progress until I caught a pair of my officers slipping on their task…much like yours used to be; to research and report. What happened to that energy? Huh? Your empathy got the best of you," Aero probed.

Master One stood up with the courage of a being who had not just been jaw shanked, and with a loud snap, he popped his jaw back into place and grinded his teeth, "at least they were progressive enough to think for themselves." Master One looked in the surrounding distance for some lethal object. Aero tired of his candor, hovered her left arm in a ceasing motion and brought him near. His body floated helplessly off the ground toward her. "I thought there was something different inside of you, One, a part of your being that *needed* change. It seemed you were most miserable after your taste of power; almost spineless," Aero whispered in his ear. The moist of her breath making him queasy.

"Mindful," One repealed her claim. He closed his eyes for some time and tried to recall a spell in spite of Aero's masterful grip around his neck.

A sharp copper stake found its way through her neck.

"Still don't need me?" Kalic huffed at Master One who was drooling blood at the mouth. Aero fell over his body like a cold blanket.

"She's   not   dead   Kalic," Master One struggled to make out. "She's not dead you fool, you only upset her." Master One, before Aero could rise from her fall, sprang from his chair and staggered across the room to his office library. He shuffled, hands uneasily waiting to retire, until he found his book of spells. Once retrieved, he tossed it across the room to Kalic; the Book of The Ascended. "Turn to the bookmark," One yelled miserably. Kalic fumbled through the book and quickly turned to the place-holder, creasing and ripping a few pages along the way. Page 305 was dense and furiously marked with ink.

"Read with haste, boy! We don't have much time before she grows conscious."

The bones in her neck cracked as she contorted herself upright. "How much do you think you'll gain by provoking me?" Aero stood up, her body transparent, reflecting everything around her. She tilted her head backward and absorbed everything but the two helpless Auralites in front of her. Master One's office became an edifice of blackness; the emptiness of their echoes consumed them.

Master One crawled around the pitch black room, not realizing that everything had been swallowed by his *maker;* an immaterial leash choked him.

"One, what did you expect?" Aero probed, "that I'd let you go on with your *Scheme* and ruin my entire operation."

"Where is the reason in cleansing entire races and extracting their identities? What are you afraid of?" One's questions pinged off the walls. Aero exhaled a static energy and a hologram appeared from the cool winds of her breath:

> Tanks reminiscent of the ones housed in the prisoner processing pipeline, were filled with hundreds of Auralites; swirling in a saturated yellow fluid. The hologram projected numerous slides of different planets and countries experiencing the same genocide

"This is larger than you and the foolish youth you've primed," Aero's voice bounced omnidirectionally and settled on the lobes of Master One and the boy. With a click of her tongue, One's office and contents were back in its place. Kalic's heart heaved up and down until his own breath was a foreign function. Without moving her lips, she spoke to Kalic, "you won't get a grown man to fall in love with you…at least not in the capacity you desire." A look of profound confusion swept over him as he tried to block psychical contact with Aero.

"The more you fight your mental, the more my presence will leach onto your suppressed energy," she reached in and sniffed Kalic's forehead, "don't think about inching near," she summoned Master One, tightening the grip around his neck. "I gave you a name, meaning to your livelihood. Power! Status! And you betray me?" Aero's grip was past deadly; veins popped from One's temples as he foamed at the mouth. She looked at him some time and for a moment a trace of hurt swept over her face. "I wouldn't let you die so easily," Aero dropped his body like a piece of scrap paper. He tried desperately to recover his faint breath; the metallic of his skin slowly appeared through patches of purple. Aero's mental enslavement ceased just enough for him to gain some emancipation. He quietly fiddled around in his coat pockets until he was reunited with the sacred wood.

She stood in awe at the young boy who knew nothing of his value; distracted. Aero waited for him to speak his mind, almost tasted the words that wanted to come from his mouth. A tear fell from Kalic's left eye. He balled his fists and stared at the book of spells patiently waiting in its place atop the bookshelf. By the grace of some God not in Aero's arsenal, Officer 1385 and 1874 appeared at ears length of the office door.

Tap Tap Tap

"Greetings, Aero, we heard some disturbances. Is everything alright?" Officer 1874 asked.

Aero invested so much of her energy tracking Kalic's and Master One's thoughts and movements, that the door knocks and subsequent voices caught her off guard. Kalic took advantage of her brief transference of conscious to use his invisibility cloak. In no time the book was in his hands, the palo santo smoke dissipated its sweetness unto the air and noses of the three. Kalic recited with urgency:

> Karmic Spell 369 was that of resurrecting Horus' spirit (*protective presence of the eye*); Master One needed Aero's eye for the Scheme Safe and so it was with Kalic's chanting of 369 and his burning of the sacred palo santo wood (*to make his enemy blind*), that Aero's eyes began to creep from the hollow pits of blackness and the whites of her eyes were begot by her pupils and the pupils of her eyes were begot by her iris and her irises were begot by her cornea, and slowly the eyeless God that was Aero, had eyes (*to be taken, of course*). Kalic retrieved the copper stake from her neck but with sudden regret, his hand was met with her tight grip.

"Kalic, your mind is too fixed on materiality," she pointed to her sight. I have lived with this darkness for some time, I can hear your heart fluttering..." Aero opened her mouth and an umbilical like chord wrapped around Kalic's neck and extended to his pineal. She kept squeezing the chord tighter around his neck, while simultaneously extracting a violet substance from his pineal gland.

"His thoughts are so true, One, you've really chosen a good successor…it's too bad he'll have to go before his prime," Aero antagonized, "it won't be long before he undergoes an underworld anesthetic, you know what will happen if his higher conscious is trapped, One." The pineal extraction sent Kalic's body into vibrating convulsions, his grip of the copper stake weakened as the melanin of his skin grew pale.

The officers crept inside without welcome and drew their lasers.

"I've never known why most hues spend much time fawning over their sensory abilities," Aero touched her newfound eyes. "There is hardly anything special about using one sense and completely disregarding the others."

She circled around the two with a fluttering clarity. "Your spells wont diminish the intent of my being," with careful hands, Aero gouged her own eyes out. Master One, jaw slacked and befuddled between love and a savior complex, leapt toward Aero, the fallen stake at Kalic's side had lost all function.

"Are these what you all want?" Aero waved the eyes in front of them, tauntingly.

"Your greed alone cannot send this boy's soul to the under-world," he staggered toward the sharpened object and swiftly placed her into a headlock.

"Drop the weapon," Officer 1385 warned Master One. Aero summoned the officers to resist, her eyes still in hand.

"Even if you kill me One, you know just as well as I do, that the spirits from the low will haunt and kill you, my followers will be here soon…you cannot hide!"

"Take the eyes," One directed Kalic who until then was in a vegetative state. Kalic trembled over to Aero and reached toward her with shaky hands, her tongue still rung around his neck. She laughed. Aero tossed her eyes into the air and with a single motion, she sliced the negative space around her and was housed in an electric field. Slouched over, she gestured her hands toward the cops and in puppeteer fashion, hovered their bodies toward her pair of eyes.

Master One and Kalic were left in a glaze, their bodies wavered in and out of a holographic frequency. This idle time did not hinder Master One's ability to generate enough psychical fuel to conjure another karmic spell. He pressed his palms together and hummed the 'e' vowel, four times, each recital greater in urgency. A long wave pierced the protective cypher around Aero and shattered her ear drum. The officers plummeted to the ground. Determination gleamed in One's eyes as he marched toward Aero, with an unrelenting force. His fist was balled tightly enough that the knife tore through his skin.

One ripped through Aero's flesh and dragged her
toward him; his eyes were as pink as the gums
hugging his teeth. Master One applied pressure to the
knife at her throat and a black thick liquid sprayed his
face. Incoherent words gurgled from her lips. At the
last stroke of Aero's threat, her umbilical cord
evaporated into silvery dust particles and Kalic was
left comatose, purple film still oozing from his
forehead.

Master One looked to the Officers, who were
knocked out cold, before he continued to make sure
his safety was ill compromised. One was already
aware that they hadn't enough energy to withstand
his and Aero's cosmic forces. He took the copper
stake and sank it repetitively into the base of her
chest cavity; desperation and freedom swept over his
manic face. Kalic stared at the limp body for some
time before realizing what had transpired.

"It's over," his words more of a question than a
statement. Master One hugged onto Kalic and
hovered a shaky blood-stained hand over his pineal
gland for thirty eye-blinks. One was trying to restore
Kalic's intuitive juices, before his soul became
property of the low. After a few failed attempts to
call him from Aero's deadly slumber, he whispered
in Kalic's ear, "just hold on…Ive got to get you into
sunlight," Master One breathed them into invisibility
and teleported cross universes to an unmarked island.

                                        (*eye blink*)

The sun was plentiful and the earth was covered in orange mud from low tidal. Even cross spatial planes, Aero's black blood stuck to their skins. "This should do it," Master One dressed Kalic's body with the salty ocean water. Purity tethered with the stains of worldly survival. One applied the same foul-smelling ointment he used to treat Kalic's contaminated ankle wound. He had chosen an island with many fruit trees for Kalic's consumption and prayed that their nutrients would nurse him back to health. It was later that night, when Kalic was slowly gaining consciousness from his intuitive coma, that Master One decided it was time to leave his side.

He prepared several servings of fruits and herbs, and left three copper keys and accompanied letters loosely, in his pant pocket. Before leaving, One held the palms of his hands to Kalic's heart and mind, transferring psychical physiognomy and memories to him. "My thoughts are yours, now, never lose these keys boy, they will open unexpected doors," Master One whispered to Kalic, there was something holding him closer to Kalic, an undeniable energy. One lifted Kalic's body so that it rested against his. He turned the young man's face and kissed his forehead, then his cheek and laid Kalic down gently on the reddened sand. "Don't let another generation live in fear," he grazed his index finger on his lips, "don't be silenced!" Kalic shifted in his sleep at One's touch. As if that were an affirmation, One evaporated from the island, from Kalic and teleported himself back to his office where the corpse of Aero had devolved into a mound of sienna ash; spell bound, only the eyes were left as well as the copper stake in one of them. The Officers were gone and One knew then, that Alphacorp officials were headed his way.

Master One carefully tiptoed to his office safe and punched in the code 5-9-7, with one wistful gesture he spun around and hovered over Aero's remains. He wasted no time searching for the eyes she had dramatically threw in the air. He only found one underneath the rubbish of her remains. Master One carefully observed the room for some time, her stale stare was soulful in the quiet of the room. He preserved the eye in a sea salt water filled container he had gathered from the unmarked island and quickly made his way to the Beta ship breaker site to open the bronze safes. When he arrived, there were hundreds of green Auralites circling the site.

"Oh   my-   ," One whispered to himself with woolly spit stuck in his throat, "I have to maintain a low profile," he said to himself. One carefully used his optical scanner to trace the entire site and finally spotted the water barrels of soiled uniforms. A few green-Auralites were transporting the barrels to a mobile cart and left the bronze safes visible. Master One knew he could not stay recluse for long, the officers were on strict watch control and each fleeting footstep made him paranoid. He decided to upkeep his authoritarian dignity and walked amongst the officers towards the safes.

"Hey Master One, I didn't see ya there?" one of the officers stated, "don't worry, we've had the whole thing on secure lock down, no one's come in or out without proper ID checks."

"Listen, I'll need you to rally up some other officers to help me move those (*pointing to the bronze safes*) to my office in the Placebo Portable, there are important documents in there that might give leads to the mass bombings..." Master One unnecessarily reasoned with the officer.

"No problem, but we have to get authorization from Aero since those are property of the underworld keeper," the officer voice-commed one of Aero's nine disciples to check in on her whereabouts. His face wrinkled at the news he received from the other end, "are you sure? That's odd, I'll have some officers go check the scene
(*pause*) yea sure, I'll keep you updated." The officer ended the voice com and re-directed his attention to Master One.

"It seems there has been no communication or updates from Aero in a few hours...and I-" Before the officer could give some bullshit excuse Master One cut in, "Listen, her missing in action is all the reason for me to get inside of those safes (*pause*) need I remind you that you answer to me if you cannot answer to Aero."

"Certainly sir, I wasn't thinking clearly, what with all the commotion and sudden attacks-, I'll have some

coppers get on them in a blink," the officer
summoned over four green Auralites to the bronze
safes; "Move these to Master One's office, they're
heavy so it may take a few rounds. Master One on
each safe transit escorted the officers to and from the
Placebo Portable. On the first visit, they all looked
down at the pile of sienna ash, quizzically and
hesitated to make any queries until the final safe 'Me'
was placed.

"So, uh…we couldn't help but notice the mountain of
ash near your desk," one of the officers pointed to the
remains while looking at the rest of the coppers.
Fortunately for Master One, Aero's clothes had
perished along with her being, "I've been attempting
to perfect a hybrid karmic spell to increase my
physical safety during this security threat…as you
can see dear Auralites, the Alphacorp dynasty is
changing…"

"Let's leave before he ashes us too," the officers
chuckled. As they departed from Master One's office,
he followed them and called out, "hey, I forgot to
mention something to you all," the officers turned
around to meet his eyes, which held all four of their
gazes, "In three eye-blinks, you will forget this ever
happened."

Master One sent violet hues, hypnotizing each of
them for a few moments until their eyes glossed over.
After a few eye blinks the officers restored their
cognizance and walked back to the nucleus of the

work site, confused at why they were in front of One's Placebo Portable.

Master One was finally able to have some moments to himself; he triple bolted his office door and closed the window blinds. Once he was in complete isolation, he unveiled the tin of seawater and removed Aero's right eye. There were harmonized clicking sounds from each safe as he held up Aero's eye to the optical scanner. At the opening of each safe, a subsequent rush of cold air escaped, placing chills on his sun kissed skin. Once opened, each safe displayed a flashing countdown from 4 minutes and 59 seconds. He wondered what would happen after the time finished. Nonetheless, there it was…all of Aero's correspondence with our planetary neighbors.

Aero had been trying for ten years to successfully colonize the Medusozoa tribe (*electric bodies with light source powers*) but the standing leaders Baba Umoja and Dr. Nia-oh were far too powerful for Aero's hacked underworld energies. Aero and her disciples were unable to manage the Medusozoans as spiritual being, so she resorted to drastic measures and caged the men of the Medusozoa underground. Her goal was to exterminate their life source as electric bodies and devolve them into Huemoons and Symptrons; hybrid, carbon copies.

After the constructed isolation of phallus and womb, Aero controlled the wombs who were

scared enough to assimilate; the rest, became pariahs
constantly in hiding of Alphacorp officials. These
outlaws of the Medusozoa tribe became known as
indixenes (*the minority group of Medusozoans*), some
of them sprinkled in different servitude camps across
the continents.

There it was in front of him three
chronologically housed bronze safes with one lengthy
document, photographs and a flash-drive in each.
Master One optically scanned all of the hard
documents and saved them to his cerebral cortex. He
then took each flash drive and inserted them into a
small opening on the inside of his left wrist. The files
loaded slowly. Three hologram folders popped up but
one entitled, Planet Oaktron, was partially encrypted
and restricted his viewing access. The Gold Coast
(planet Hegemorph) and Meditron's firewalls were
easier to get through. Master One updated the
findings to his cerebral hard-drive with a single touch
to his right temple. His fingers stretched along the
smooth finish of each bronze safe.

Safe, *Sc* (*Study and Coagulate*), contained
contents ranging between the years 2975-2985 BD.
The file was 97 pages long and seemed to be notes
from various meetings that were outlining blueprints
for the Alphacorp ethnic cleansing. Apparently, Aero
had made several visits before the year 2795, offering
trade unions of advanced technology in exchange for
natural minerals. Aero and her disciples made
unsuccessful attempts to copper wire Medusozoan
leaders of Meditron, the only communication they

could rely on were hearsay from neighboring townsfolk. There were a multitude of pages allocated to the architecture of the planet and redevelopment blueprints cross countries. The flash drive contained a series of contacts and their geographical coordinates.

(01:52 flashed on all three safes)

Master One scrambled to look through the second set of files. Safe, *He* (*Hover and Enterprise*), ranged between the years 2985-2995 BD, and was devoted to the infiltration of religion on both groups. Within the file, there were minutes pertaining to Alphacorp gentrifying:

> "To live among a people, to build an economy among said people, and to breed with these people, are direct methods for controlling said people"
> -   X

(00:58 flashed on all three safes)

By this time, Master One was sweating; he reached for the third safe's flash drive, *Me* (*Manifest and Evolve*), and inserted it into his hard drive. Master One's jaw gaped at the images of mass human slaughtering and notes of an underground incarceration that spanned between 2995-3005 AD. Master One tried to piece together each finding into a single narrative of events. He was unsure of what would happen once the time ended on all three safes,

he shoved all three flash drives up his anal cavity. He
sat uneasy for a while and called into Kalic's psyche.

Beep Beep...Beep Beep...Beep Beep...

"Come on Kalic, wake up!" Master One continued to
reach his only saving grace, finally Kalic answered,
his mind still seemed to be recuperating from his
unfinished pineal extraction.

"You were right, the details matter," Kalic chuckled
carefully. Master One silenced Kalic's aching banter
and recited brief descriptions of each safe, like an
auctioneer.

"Remember the sequence, Kalic"...

(00:07 flashed on all three safes)

"30 years of conditioning and they didn't even gain
access to the hover-" Master One's last audible words
before the bronze safes detonated. Kalic squeezed his
eyes tightly, holding onto the sand underneath him.
The high pitched frequencies coming from Master
One's network gave Kalic a pressure headache.

Scene 7

Before Valerian could step into the Placebo
Portable, she was grabbed by two green Auralites,
and barely had time to process Master One's office
ablaze, he hoped that Kalic wasn't in there.

"Where are you taking me?" She questioned the cops
while kicking and squirming in their tight grip.

"We will do the questioning! Why were you standing
outside of One's office? Where were you in the last
1000 eye-blinks?"

Va showed them the Beta-medic band on her wrist
and said she had been in one of the mass bus
bombings. She lifted her shirt to show the two
officers her scars. After a while the officers knew she
wouldn't give them the answers they were hoping
for.

"I was on my way to Master One to ask him for some
of his healing ointment to dress my wounds," she
convincingly lied. The Auralites took her to the line
of Betas awaiting their copper chip pineal implants.

"Wait! What the f-" Va couldn't get the rest of her
worry out before the cops were out of sight.
Alphacorp scientists were going down the line of
Betas and injecting them with a functioning
anesthesia to numb their faces for procedure. Patient
malpractice and negligence the least of their worries,
as they wished to orchestrate what was left of the

Alphacorp mission. Valerian scoped her surroundings for an exit; entrance to refuge.

***

Kalic woke up the following day to the whirring sounds of shallow ocean currents washing over his torso; confused by his tropical surroundings, he reached into the red earth and held it up to the lemon yellow light. His recollection of yesternight was foggy, the only thing he was sensible of was the burning sensation around his neck and forehead. Kalic stood up to stretch, his equilibrium was thrown off by a surge of inner visions. He thought of Master One and almost suddenly three bronze safes appeared before the skeletal wall of his mind. His had throbbed as he walked toward the ocean and skipped stones.

"Where is he?" Kalic asked himself.

There was no sign of human civilization in his immediate vantage point. Mango and jackfruit trees loomed just before the ocean. Kalic sat for a few moments trying to recall how he got there and Master One's whereabouts. He planted his feet on the reddened earth and focused on the weight of his right pants leg; he reached in his pocket and found three copper keys.

"That's odd," he muttered aloud. Metal keys had long since been recalled, once policy-makers realized it was a wasted energy source. After a few eye blinks and nauseating head pains, Kalic received another vision of the safes exploding and a tight knot cradled his esophagus. The sun's incandescence peeled at Kalic's dry melanin and so he huddled under the nearby mango tree.

"I've got to get the fuck off this island."

It seemed like it took trillions of eye blinks before Kalic rested his gaze on a potential hover portal made of the sun; instead he decided to wait for night's moon and observed if it was an alternate hover portal. Once the cool settled, Kalic used some hover fuel and activated Karmic lesson 123; flight. He stretched his arms in repeated windmill motions, his body reverberated. In 98 consecutive arm windmills, Kalic's body was above the ground, he made his way toward the moon. Karmic spell 123 and his hover fuel gave out on him just two klicks away, he was swallowed by the ocean.

The sea water engulfed all of his being, his vision was confined to blue-green tones, tiny air bubbles escaped from his nose and mouth against the waters. As he drowned he thought of the cleansing ceremonies with Va; how it always seemed to feel like she was baptizing him, cleaning the parts she sought to fix...*caught up in the rapture*. Kalic allowed the chaotic waters to take over and remembered to surrender his body to the ocean and float with the waves. He managed to ease himself back ashore, where he continued his arm windmills, this time, increasing the amount by 23.

Kalic's second attempt at Karmic lesson 123 allowed him access to the moon's portal, as cold as it appeared, his skin seared. It was important that Kalic focused on his desired location. Once conscious of the other side, he realized his surroundings; the Beta ship breaker work site. There were green Auralites patrolling the entire site, so Kalic could only make out the bare minimum of happenings. The yellow caution tape streaming around Master One's Placebo Portable grabbed his gaze. Beta-medics removed severed body parts from his office, one by one, via body stretchers. Knots formed in Kalic's throat and he regurgitated a purple film of saliva. He managed to keep himself away from One's door and followed the voices of the townspeople, to avoid being interrogated. Beta hues screamed hysterically in terror, Kalic was able to decipher bits on the bombings and the deaths of Aero and Master One. Acidic mango juice crept up his throat and left a bittersweet taste.

Within a few hours, all the Betas had to undergo a series of lie detector tests, skin samples and re-identification branding through copper implants. Until the recent killings of the Alphacorp leaders, Betas were full bodied humans; at the onset of the Alphacorp devolution, each Beta was implanted with copper chips at the fore of their heads. The governing officials were fearful of another terrorist attack and used the pineal chips as a system to track Beta brains.

Kalic had to get to the ambulance to see One's corpse. He crept behind a Beta-medic on the side of Master One's office and strangled him to the floor with unforgiving hands. Kalic took a few moments before he realized the man was dead, possessed by some guised self. Sweat slipped off his chin and his breath upcycled into dry heaves. He quickly undressed the Beta-medic and slipped on his clothes. Kalic stuffed the naked cadaver into an empty water barrel and remembered to get the three copper keys from his pants' pocket before throwing his old clothes into the stream of chemical waste.

Kalic walked over to the van and studied the burnt body and gathered his emotional strength before entering. Almost suddenly, he received an inner vision of Master One planting flash drives into his anus. The thought of reaching into a burnt asshole, did nothing less than disturb Kalic; however, he did not shy away from a final chance of closure with One. He opened the door, quickly uncovered the black sheet from One's body and reached inside his anus. "This isn't how I imagined our first time," Kalic tried to make necrophilic sense of an ironically intimate moment. It didn't take him more than 9 eye-blinks to feel out the three flash drives; he pulled them out one by one and thought nothing of the brown excrements on each drive as he stuffed them into his pants' pocket. There was no time to wash his hands. Kalic stepped out of the van and dusted himself off. He moved toward the exit of the Beta ship breaker work site, and without looking back, made his way to Va.

Once Kalic arrived at Va's compound, he was surprised to see the door wide open and no one in sight. The radio blared news about the droves of captured Betamorphs. Kalic turned on the television and noticed the province-wide broadcasting of the Beta ship breaker site. Each station displayed thousands of people being synched to controlling systems. He remembered the flux of polyviduals at the Beta site and figured Va was right along with everyone else. An urgency washed over him, he walked out the door with a particular conviction and headed back to the central district.

Scene 8

Hundreds of Auralites were sectioned
between two columns with the neon signs; Huemoon
and Symptron. Each gathered frantically in lines, no
one noticed Kalic slip pass the green Auralite
officials. It was almost Va's turn to receive the
anesthetic, she began fiddling with her chewed
fingertips. As soon as the Alphacorp doctor reached
in and touched her forehead, Va grabbed the doctor's
dominant hand holding the syringe and placed her
into an abrupt choke hold; the syringe was now at the
doctor's neck.

"Don't fucking move, or I'll jam this whole syringe
up the side of your neck!" Va said daring the
approaching cops to try her.

"Listen to the young woman, all the other scientists
and doctors have been demoted or killed. I'm the
only one who knows the control system. If you make
any moves, we will all live to regret this," the doctor
reasonably ordered the green Auralites to stand
down. "You can't get away with this outburst for too
long, young woman, what do you plan to do?" the
sweet motherly voice of the doctor, knowingly
probed Va. Va discerned their bodies out of the ship
breaker site, the green Auralites suspiciously
followed behind.

"You don't really have a plan, eh?" chuckled the
doctor. Still keeping her in a choke-hold, Va searched
their surroundings and spotted a purple hue hovering

in the distance behind some trash bins. It was a
familiar energy. At this moment of mysterious
comfort, she took her right hand, holding the syringe,
and stabbed the doctor in her neck. The needle
shattered inside of her flesh, a surge of tiny purple
veins outlined the doctors neck and face. The green
Auralites came charging toward Va, their submachine
guns beaming variant red lasers on her body. Out of
thin air, Va was thrusted from off the ground, she
looked down at the shooting officers.

"It's me," Kalic whispered in her ear, "what kind of
foolishness were you trying to pull down there? You
could have been killed!"

"I'm not dead yet," she hugged onto him tighter,
under the invisibility cloak.

"We need to get to the forest and stay there for a few
nights, then find a trail South, we are fugitives now,"
Kalic pressed his hands on Va's waist.

"Good thing we don't have copper implants, yet," she
horribly assured him. Before night fell, they were in
an eastern rain forest; swampy earth leeched onto
their lower bodies.

EXTENSION II

The

Marsh

"We are settling in moist."

The muddy water is desolate. Only when wind blows, do the waves of marsh ripple. The sun is hiding behind trees. The trees are tall and hunched over, telling the time. The wind whispers a cool heat; like an elder's breath, or like the scent of aged wood. The birds no longer chirp in a frenzy, they instead, sing at the rise of each hour; letting souls know when it is time to prey.

The earth slopes in all directions and in the nucleus, there forms an inverse apex, it is marshy. Just beyond the dense slush is a portal. The portal's accessibility depended on the amount of sunlight accrued throughout a given day. Any being who dared to enter, could only exit upon careful maturation of will.

Beneath the portal's sheath is a green funnel-like cave; two bodies are found, stuck in hibernation. One of them consists of only the upper half, while the other, only the lower half.

Mushrooms grow from the green tunnel; the two bodies lie on them for comfort and ingest them for medicinal and nutritional purposes. It has been 4796 hours; their only awareness of time are through laborious lights and dense darks. The upper body's crown vines to the peak of the green portal, while the lower body's feet root deeply into marshy earth. They must find themselves in one another. The upper body carefully extracts some of the mushroom's juice onto their skin and aids the lower body in moisturizing itself. Once closer, raw muscle tissue crept from the nerve endings on each half. They found comfort for 504 hours, their muscles healing a once severed life.

On the 5300th hour, the two bodies, conjoin into one and are spat upward from the green portal and onto the marsh; naked and soiled.

Once probed into the new space, they crawled around observing every detail, adjusting their eyes to the sun, marveling in the new feeling of their joint body. To their right, a woman appeared, naked and laying on a throne of mushrooms. She waited for the body to come to her and with each inch forward, the enthroned lady moved near.

"You are here"

…and the two bodies, now one, only knowing language through rhythm and embrace, clicked the tongue and groped the mushrooms around the woman's lower body. This act summoned the birds. The birds cyphered around the three entities, now two, cooing and hovering. The wind from their wings, whistled the grass. The sun starts to rise and fall, synchronically and the tree walls rise higher and higher; taking shape over them.

The sun sinks and melts their skin into waves absorbing into the marshy earth under them. The sun bursts into black chips of geometric molecules. Their skin evaporates into waves, an essence rises and dissipates.

A tiny flash-drive lay on the marsh

8 hours later, a tribe of three walk along the woody trail. There is no marsh, just firm soil and clusters of trees clumping thickness. The tribe consists of Symptrons; chimeras of android and humanoid breeding, conducted by scientists of the Alphacorp dynasty; two hue wombs and one xem (gender non-conforming hue).

"My energy is nearing depletion, I haven't smelt or seen anybody since our last stop," Zaas whines to the others.

"Sh, Sh…I can feel something," Knowl looked at the two lovers with conviction.

"Those birds rushed South of us, hours ago. We may very well be walking in circles, Knowl," Cosma contributed.

"Birds don't fly South for no reason, especially during this Spring season. Some force pulled them. I feel-"

"Your intuition has led us amuck for eight hours! We have spent more energy searching for the unknown than using our internal gps to put us back on the grid," Zaas increased her pitch.

Soft murmurs crept in the near distance of the tribe who all turned to each other for reassurance of their own sanity. Knowl was the first of the trio who advanced toward the sounds.

"We were closer than we thought," Knowl stepped from behind a tall oak tree and found the couple, naked, with limbs overlapped.

The womb rode aggressively atop the fragility of the man's body, it was he who exhaled the soft cries. Their smell was dank amidst the putrid earthy tones of mushrooms that lie beside them. The young man clawed his gritty nails into the skin of her back; similar scabs were found in proximity. She fed off this pain and pulled him deeper, her hips shaking as she thrusted back and forth. They both groaned for some time, shaking, before the man noticed the three strangers, watching and gently pushed the woman off of him.

He stood; erect and exposed. He cleared his throat, looked at the others in awe and used a memorized karmic spell to scan them for weapons.

"At ease, Va, they don't have any harmful weapons on them...go grab our belongings," he waited for her and stared at the three with his brow raised.

"Were you all not going to state your presence?" "W-w-we (cough) WE haven't seen other Huemoons and symptrons in over a week, post devolution of Alpha-Corp," Cosma spoke for the tribe.

"A week?" Kalic scratched his head, the graze of Va's hands caught him off guard, "You startled me," he smiled at his beloved.

"This is my partner, Valerian, I am Kalic," he said to the three and attempted to extend his hand almost forgetting of the moments prior.

"You two don't have the typical third dreyeve optical scanners, like the rest of us," Knowl pointedly stated, "and uh, not to mention those," they chuckled to the group.
Kalic looked down at his testicles and rose stained the brown of his skin.

"Fortunately, we were able to bypass their procedures. They've controlled us for too long, but not our seeds," he looked to Valerian and smiled.

"Must be nice operating on an outdated system. MindFeeder agents have managed to nearly brainwash the entire country to disassociate us from our home. What is planet Hegemorph anyway!" Knowl skeptically stared through Kalic's physical being as everyone laughed cautiously.

"Are there any more of you?" Zaas specifically questioned Valerian.

"We've only seen the occasional cola zomb through these forests," she reached for their belongings and handed Kalic his garments. "The only weapons we got are our minds and these herbs," she waved to the surrounding nature. I'm certain, if you all were able to find us, a trained professional will track us in no time," Valerian added a stark reality.

"How do we know y'all aren't crazy? You're the ones with metal transplants...here to kill us, eh?" Kalic keenly observed them.

"Easy, we're no more a threat than the two of you. It only took the fall of our people, to invoke a change within," Zaas looked to her two tribeskin.

"Oddly enough, you look familiar," Cosma pointed at Kalic, "your face was," she snapped her fingers and strained to recall her memory. "Ah! You're the man from the news, right?" Cosma's fan-girling was quickly overcome with anxiety. "You're the new pariah of Alphacorp, you assaulted a cop just before Aero's death." Kalic finished clothing himself and adjusted into an easy posture. Both parties studied the other over for some time, but Kalic hardly wavered his firm stance.

"Anyone whose had a hand in dismantling our screwed system is alright with me," Knowl extended their wrist to Kalic for an exchange. In spite of their skepticism the others followed suit; the synchronization heightened the energies as a collective force.
"Now we each can access cerebral communication without external interference," Knowl assured the tribe.

"Where's the rest of your people?" Kalic sternly asked.

"The reconstruction of Alphacorp into planet Hegemorph created a lot of chaos. Auralites were so accustomed to their mental programming that when the new leaders took over, there were disruptions throughout the entire planet. A lot of them were drugged by the MindFeeder gang and shipped to servitude camps. The folks who successfully got away are probably scrounging for survival, like us. We decided to break off into smaller groups to avoid being a spectacle," Zaas shared.

"To be honest, we've lasted this long on sheer faith and it seems we were destined to find you all," Cosma gestured to Valerian and Kalic.

"The other members of our group left on some inclination of refuge in the opposite direction of Meditron…but there was something pulling us south," Zaas continued.

The five trudged for some time before recognizing the rainbow sorbet melting behind the horizon. Kalic noticed their energies shift into a survival state. Goosebumps tempted his tired skin, " this has been our post for the last 20 hours, you all are the first travelers we've encountered…we're safe," his words echoed like isolated affirmations, that eased their tensions.

Each of them began scanning their immediate surroundings for lodging. MindFeeders are most active during the evenings when they can easily hack their target's conscious. Although in recluse, the group is more vulnerable as a collective energy source.

One of the hikers feels a hardened surface under their foot. She picks up the flash drive and notices its sleek copper body and the intricate lines and numbers inscribed into the metal. Cosma shares her finding to the group.

"What are the odds?" Cosma inserts the chip into her wrist drive and begins scanning the file.

"Holy Hellatron," she gasps.

"What is it Cosma?" Zaas called out to her.

"I think this is the missing hover-link between us and a larger presence…there are scrolls of numbers, symbols and links to images that aren't downloading to my junk-drive. I can't make out the language, it seems to pre-date the current lingual processor on my drive."

"Let me take a look at that chip, I just updated my software and should have some space," Zaastria grazed Cosma's hand as she reached for the copper chip and inserted it into her reader.

"Holy Hellatron doesn't even begin to tack this...the images are still foggy but I can make only one ancient Meta-Sh word; Nut...also known as the Sky Goddess" Zaastria looked to Cosma and the rest of the group, reflectively. "What I'm gathering suggests that the war between Alphacorp and Meditron was parasitic."

"Isn't that a generational happening?" Knowl offered their indifference.

"True, however the leaders of Meditron thought Aero's threats to be juvenile in the judgement of the Higher World and therefore the scales were left unbalanced...Hey Kalic don't you know a Master One?" Zaas asked.

"Uh...yea, how-?" Kalic hesitated before answering his own question and looked at his wrist.

"His name along with a Baba Umoja and Dr. Nia-oh, keeps showing up throughout the document, there are scrolls of consistent communication between all three of them" Zaas said.

"Baba Umoja and Dr. Nia-oh were notorious rebels of the Medusozoa tribe. They, too, were slain by Alphacorps who established a Betamorph camp in Meditron," Knowl hummed knowingly.

"Whatever they did, or knew, killed them...You could have been right there with him Kalic" Va whispered.

"Don't start this again Va, it's been at least a month since the devolution; besides, it'll take more than a nuclear war to split us up," Kalic sent a kiss to Va's lips.

"Before the devolution, One gave me access to his memories..." Kalic reached into his breast pocket and lingered on the thought of Master One for a while.

"Anything noteworthy?" Cosma asked.
"I haven't found any alarming news," white lies trickled from his lips as surely as the blood coursing through his veins.

"How are we going to decipher the rest of the notes?" Zaastria asked the group.

Knowl replied, "There's a few indixene Medusozoa descendants in Meditron about 1500 klicks south of the Gold Coast, they have knowledge of the old language, *Meta-Sh*. From how Zaas is describing the notes, it resembles their systems of embedding numeric and symbolic scrolling."

"Let's get going on the trail tonight, we'll have to be weary of the active MindFeeders...with our numbers we can manage," Kalic affirmed.

"If we have enough provisions to last a week, we can provide an offering to the elders and hopefully be welcomed," Knowl said. "Perhaps we could offer them seeds, showing our interest in fruiting with them," said Cosma.

A quiet settled over the group as they rummaged through their belongings. A red haze moved beyond the trees until they were engulfed by probing stars. Valerian initiated comfort on a nearby stoop which provoked the others to join. As easiness dispersed amongst the Trillage, their dialogue smoothed into conversation. Organic.

Zaas looked to Cosma, then Knowl, and stared reluctantly at the couple across from them.

"I think we've all been avoiding a larger question. How'd you two miraculously survive the Devolution and claim that it's been over a year? Its barely, been two weeks " Zaas leant closer to Kalic and Valerian, nose curled, daring to smell a lie. "I mean, am I the only one questioning the motives of these two?" Zaas looked to Cosma and Knowl for reassurance; their silence lingered in the thick air before Cosma offered some level-headed energy to the Trillage, "for all we know, they're a blessing, Zaastria...loosen up, we have to find a hover shuttle soon, use your conspiring energy to focus!"

Mind slumber almost begot them until Kalic sprung to his feet, "we can sort out the details during our journey."

Kalic + Va (*Lover-lude*)

It was hot; there was snow scraping dog shit
pavement, as idle bodies lie anxiously unveiling
worlds within careful touches. Because hell was cold
and only a few multividuals akin to heaven's ascent
remained; skins crackled into blisters via this fiery
ice. The passion settled over bloodied box wine and
peeled lips. Cannibalistic measures taken to restore
the ignorance of western fore-fathers were erupted as
Kalic bit Va's lips. To say that neither of them were
acting out their truest selves, would be a mockery.

"I have only this scar tissue to offer you, it comes
packed with cytoplasmic fuel to domino effect this
parasitic catalyst. Can't you see my scramble for
words?"

And so, it was the age old fable which forewarned
seeds of neglected trees, that even in destruction, a
cure could splinter. Neither what, nor who, could
recollect that moment when their vice became their
virtue.

"We stand before one another, this I am sure your
eyes can see; wounded. There are distant imprints of
chains folding themselves onto your ankles and feet.
How could you manage?"
And as if the other body knew the repercussions of
answering such a blatant question, she did not answer
and she only looked; pessimistic and quizzical. By
this time, their two bodies were intertwined and
ethers sent pulsating wavelengths throughout their

domains. Kalic traced her spiraling branch scars from her right hip to her to the left of her neck. Who is to say that a rapture in the chest does not match that of feathers pulling butterflies throughout the stomach?

Va whispered, "why do you find it necessary to speak?"

"Because you trusted me, even when I chose Master One, you waited throughout my naivety, you salvaged me through ruins…"

"I realized that I could never salvage the whole you; we've nurtured one another and now look…even in destruction, what with the world almost ending, we are here. Together.
We know why you chose Master One, he saved the grace that was stolen from you. I waited because I never wanted to change you… I hoped that one day you would come to me, as I came to you"

"I think about him from time to time…the look in his eyes, it still haunts me"

EXTENSION III

Ply
Rise of the Medusozoan
Mouth

(Meanwhile on the neighboring planet, a pit-guar growls as two women draw near)

Elder Womb:
If we don't shut this breed up, the guards will catch onto us. We mustn't lose our guise

Veiled Womb:
We can give it the special meat

(Veiled Womb reaches into her side satchel and comes up with neatly packaged brown wax paper)

Elder Womb:
Be careful not to give it too much because we still need plenty for the guards

(Veiled Womb tosses three slivers of pig meat to the chimera who heartily devours the meat before it had time to settle on the red soil)

Elder Womb:
Give it a moment to spread

(The Elder Womb covered her nose in dismay of the foul blood-stricken meat. The two wombs continued dragging through the heat, their golden skin matching the glaze of the ripened mangos hanging from crouching branches. The prison compound was known for their fresh produce and was not shy on selling the fruits of their prisoner's labor. The Elder Womb reached for an avocado and placed it meticulously in her bag, crimson plums followed)

Veiled Womb:
Look there, the second entry gate is just ahead and
smoke seems to be coming from the compound…

Elder Womb:
It seems we have come during mealtime. The meat
won't be so random now. Walk slowly, I think there
are watch dogs circling the compound

*(Elder Womb closes her eyes and zones in on the
direction of the sounds; she motions for her daughter
to go in the opposite direction and check out the
premises)*

> **Guard A:**
> I feel something approaching

> **Guard B:**
> Oh yea? Did you smoke on your break
> again? You know that reefer will pull a
> number on you

> *(Guard B pulls a flask from their deerskin
> trousers and chuckles faintly)*

> **Guard A:**
> No, no, it's another presence

> **Guard B:**
> It could just be the pit-guars, take a smoke
> stick

(The two wombs, now crouching, moved to the rear of the compound)

Veiled Womb:
Mama, the gate is cracked over here, lets slip through and find an entry point to the main compound.

(The two wombs travel lightly through the gate, their bodies seem to malleate to the twisted opening)

I'm checking those doors to our right. Osu told me they usually keep one of the exit doors unlocked for breaks

Elder Womb:
Be careful, a lot of changes have been made since Baba…don't step into a trap

(Veiled Womb goes to the door and thrusts the handle)

Veiled Womb:
No budge, but look up there

(pointing to an open window)

but how will I get up there?

Elder Womb:
You can tie the vines from the trees to your body and use the grooves of the stucco compound to climb

(as they fumbled the vines in knots, the Elder Womb revealed a sleek silver blade from beneath her tongue, she carefully wiped it off and handed it to her daughter)

Here, use this

Veiled Womb:
You never cease to amaze me…If I don't make it back in thirty minutes, you know what to do

(They both knowingly shook their heads; the Elder Womb grabbed the Veiled womb's face and kissed her forehead)

Go now, I will keep my eyes and ears open. If you run into any trouble, whistle our code and I will signal an alarm to distract the officials

**

(There was blood funneling down the Veiled womb's arms and hands as she managed her weight through the cracked glass window. The little drops of scarlet trailed her throughout the tanned floors of the compound. She followed the aroma of skewered meat to the meal room)

Guard C:
Hey!
Hey, you!
Ay, miss! Where do you think you're going?

(The Guard power walks in her direction)

Veiled Womb:
Oh, pardon me, I didn't hear you. I'm trying to locate
the meal room, I have some food for my loved ones

Guard C:
Why are you coming from the second floor? How'd
you get past the guards with that crap on your face?
Why are you bleeding? Who are you?
Hey, miss, look at me when I'm addressing you!
Who are you?

Veiled Womb:
I am Kujichagulia. I've come bearing dried foods and
meat for my loves.

Guard C:
Why are you bleeding?

*(His stale breath clung to the Veiled womb's nostrils,
he began circling around her grunting, pulling at the
pockets of his trousers)*

Veiled Womb:
One of the watchdogs bit me and so-

Guard C:
Which watchdog?

Veiled Womb:
I, I can't quite recall, it was big and ivory stained

Guard C:
They all are, you'll have to do better than that

Veiled Womb:
I, I...

Guard C:
Listen miss, a few things could happen; you could
either let me clean you up, or be taken to the
trespassing camp
(He circled back in front of her face)

What's it gonna be?

Veiled Womb:
I'm just here to feed and see my loves

Guard C:
That's the wrong answer

*(The guard grabbed at the womb's head veil and
pulled back in dismay at the sight of the face. The
guard while tumbling over, quivered at the symbols)*

Y...you... you're from the Medusozoa Tribe! But I
thought-

Kujichagulia:
We were all extinct?
*(The scars stretched from above the womb's right eye
and her tentacles spiraled to her solar plexus, as the
veil fell gracefully to the ground)*

We wanted to keep a low profile, if you are wise, you won't yell for backup

(The now unveiled womb slowly approached the guard and whispered in his ear)
Where do you keep the prisoners?

Guard C:
But there was chemical warfare on your race...the effects were supposed to be irreversible...

(The unveiled womb touched the base of her scar. The touch ignited a conductive force, illuminating the scar and tentacles to a scarlet tint. She touched his left cheek and slowly released electrodes. His skin sizzled...)

Guard C:
AHHHH! JEES-

Kujichagulia:
I do not have time to fill you in on the pitfalls of the Alphacorp complex. Where are the prisoners?

Guard C:
Im not afraid of you people, you're an abomination, a disease

Kujichagulia:
If I touch you, you will die

Guard C:
OFFICERS! OFFICERS!
HELP! HELP! THERES AN—

*(Before the guard could finish his last words, the
unveiled womb melted his entire left cheek with an
electric current, reached in and grabbed his tongue.
The frequency provoked body spasms and foamy
saliva crept from the guard's mouth. By the time she
was done, his tongue resembled a shriveled piece of
bacon, his eyes widened and glossed over)*

Kujichagulia:
Can it all be so simple?

*(She reached for and assembled her head dress and
darted to the nearest electrical outlet and stuck both
fingers into the power socket. The prison compound
blacks out, causing an eruption in all the occupants.
An employee speaks over the intercom ordering for
Guards to close down the compound and search the
premises.*

> *Meanwhile the Elder Womb traipses the
> premises for a discrete place to wait for her
> daughter. She heard the alarms send out a
> reticent cry and knew that Kujichagulia had
> little time before officials would be
> searching every nook and cranny. Just
> before she reached the thorny blackberry
> bushes for cover, an unbearable pain shot
> from her vagina and settled at her feet. She
> yelped before her knees caved to the soil.*

*She fought the pain and dug deeper into the
earth before a voice reached her)*

Elder Womb:
You must be in some trouble to access
psychokinesis with no forewarning
gesture…

Citronella:
I couldn't wait for your call

Guard A:
Get the dogs, I think we've got an intruder

*(Before the lights went out, a walkie message came in
from one of the internal patrolling guards. Guard B
noticed a trail of blood on the second floor leading to
the control room. He went to check it out, but hasn't
confirmed anything over the station yet)*

Guard A:
Alert the other guards and check on the head officer.
Let's get the emergency lock on the prison gates,
now!

Guard B:
Copy

*(The Veiled womb now at the door of the control unit,
kicked the door in and found the head officer sitting
patiently in the dark)*

Officer:

I knew it was only a matter of time before you people crawled from under your rocks

Veiled Womb:
You mean your people

(the officer dismissed the veiled wombs claim with a snarl)

Where have you all been hiding, we sent search squads to every province in the country. Each citizen was implanted with nano-chips and documented. How could you all escape?

Veiled Womb:
Where are they?

Officer:
Don't you want to at least humor me, since you barged in unannounced?

(The Officer stood up from her chair and walked around her desk to face the Veiled Womb)

Even with that veil, I can still see inside of you Kuji, nothing's changed.

Veiled Womb:
I don't have time for the back and forth banter with you Xora. Where are they?

Officer:
Oh, you mean your impregnators, testes... phallics?
Why do you want to know? You wombs have
managed for so long without them...

Veiled Womb:
You know why, Xora

Officer:
That's not my name

*(The Veiled womb leaned past the Officer and lit
their desk lamp with her index finger. She could hear
the cringe of Xora's bones)*

Veiled Womb:
You could have still been one of us, had you not sold
your soul to fit the image of your oppressor. It
sickens me to notice the waste you've become

*(The Veiled womb reached in and touched the
Officer's bleached skin)*

You can't cover them Xora, I still see your scars
underneath this new skin, this new mask

Officer:
Y'know what makes me sick- is how you could hover
in here after seven years and think your power is
enough to defeat an entire system. Minds have been
programmed! Minds! You know what comes after a
people forget to think for themselves?...

Veiled Womb:
Answer me!

Officer:
They are underground

(she pointed her fingers in a cyclic fashion)

We knew the one way to slowly break what was left of your tired race down; the absence of electricity, of nature, of a life source…

Veiled Womb:
Then you know I will do any and everything necessary to restore justice

(The Officer chuckled to herself, a wince of pain underneath her confident façade)

Officer:
Invisibility doesn't suit you, Kuji. You were always so bold, so unwilling to bend at the customary hem of femininity…your eyes were always watching

(The Officer traced her index finger along the wooden finish of her desk as she found her way in front of Kujichagulia)

We could have been a great force

(Kujichagulia cleared her throat and strained to see the truth. She slowly unveiled the head scarf and exposed her tentacles. Xora reached to touch her face

and for a moment, Kuji felt the easy sting of old embers)

Kujichagulia:
If this were six years ago, I'd melt over this lazy gesture…but you chose your allegiance

(With a zap of her finger, the lights were back on throughout the prison compound. Kujichagulia leapt toward Xora and pressed her lips against hers.

Electric energy accumulated.

Kujichagulia dived in the forbidden pleasure and tried desperately to block out all the misery Xora had caused her people. This time, she knew she had to disfigure Xora's image and accept her for who she was; an Alphacorp Officer.

The Officer's body convulsed spasmodically and with each electric shock, pools of saliva foamed from her mouth. Kujichagulia noticed speckles of translucent film in the Officer's saliva and pried open her mouth with both hands.   Snap
*   The Officer's mandibular region cracked open and left her lower jaw sagging. Kujichagulia pulled at the Officer's lingual membrane and dug down her throat. There was a slick rigid panel at the back of her trachea. The Officer struggled to yell, only monotone mumbles managed to escape her cries. Kujichagulia fumbled around the Officer's desk for something sharp to gouge the panel out. Before she could*

manage, a group of guards rushed into the control unit)

Guard E:
What in the universe do you think you're doing to our...our-

(Guard E gasps and tries to hold vomit; five other guards subsequently rush in after him with MP5 Ks aimed directly at the Veiled Womb)

Guard F:
Get on the fucking ground, NOW!

(Guards G-J circle around Kujichagulia attempting to close her in. Guard F managed to grip Kujichagulia's neck with both hands but before she could be contained, her body radiated an intoxicating red hue and pulsated rhythmically as the electric friction accumulated. Guard F's hands were electrified from her high voltage, which made it impossible for him to release his grip.
                              He was dead in five seconds.
She   gestured   to   the rest   of   the   guards)

Kujichagulia:
I hate to make examples out of you all...

(She drew in three deep breaths and with both palms culminated a circular-energetic-current, which she then directed at each guard, electrocuting them)

I will find them, Xora

(Kujichagulia searched one of the Guards and found a pocket knife- she then proceeded to dig the panel out of the Xora's throat. It was a sleek copper flash drive)

If you still have enough spirit in you, Xora, you shall live and remember the damnation you caused to your own people.

(The translucent film of blood spilt from the officer's mouth and throat, her eyes teared up as she watched the Veiled Womb walk away... Kujichagulia left the control unit and went to the first floor of the compound, the ceilings' solar lights flickered as the sun set and she knew it was well past thirty minutes. She kept searching the compound for clues because her mother hadn't signaled a warning. Kujichagulia found a stairwell leading to a lower level)

Kujichagulia:

(talking to herself)

It's so dark in here, the air smells like the oceans moist algae and spoilt blood

(Kujichagulia used her retinal intuit processor to activate night vision. There were scraps of brass metal and skeletal bones on the floor bed. As she kept walking along the narrow path, the stench of blood and bodily excrements pervaded her senses. It was

not just the thickness of soiled blood that permeated the womb...)

Ghostly Phallic:
Is it war you're searching for?

(She quickly reassembled her head scarf and answered the disgruntled voice)

Veiled Womb:
Who's there?

(Pause)

Greetings!?

(Pause)

Who's there?

Ghostly Phallic:
...You won't get anywhere demanding answers

Veiled Womb:
It's just...the dark is blinding...and there are so many frantic and unsettled voices

Ghostly Phallic:
Don't you know the voices of your ancestors? Have you been that far removed from your culture?
We have been waiting for someone of your kind
Veiled Womb:

My kind?   Waiting…for what…for
who?

Ghostly Phallic:
You.
Your blood-
We can smell its' sweet salt, like that of the Atlantic
Ocean
Can you not smell it?

(*Kujichagulia now crouched over squatting, listening
to the earth below her*)

Veiled Womb:
I noticed it when I first walked in the dungeon

Ghostly Phallic:
It's yours

Veiled Womb:
But I am not bleeding…

(*Kujichagulia proceeded in touching her body*)

Ghostly Phallic:
There's no use in searching for the physical blood, it
continuously spills. The blood is in your body, it
flows from your womb. The blood is a product of
massacre. You smell it because it is now in you, the
blood of the voices you here…their blood is in you

Veiled Womb:
But I've only now smelt this…this blood

Ghostly Phallic:
You've reactivated your connection to us. We are
your spirit guides, when you opened the door to this
cellar, you opened your soul to us, you released us
from staying housed underground

Veiled Womb:
Our phallic members have been gone for seven years
now, only our wombs are left

Ghostly Phallic:
We have been here

Veiled Womb:
Why weren't you able to stop them?

Ghostly Phallic:
They caught us off guard, we are not killers by
nature. They studied us, knew our weaknesses,
threatened your lives unless we surrendered. No
foresight could have prepared us for such greed

Veiled Womb:
I am Kujichagulia, daughter of Queen Mother
Nostalgia and Baba Umoja

(*She knelt to the ground and revealed her scars and
tentacles*)

I am humbled by your grace. May I ask who I have the pleasure of speaking with?

Ghostly Phallic:
We are family, Kuji, stand and hold your head high. I am called Dr. Nia-oh…wipe the despair from your face, for our faith still exists

Kujichagulia:
We need to multiply, we are facing extinction and the elders are passing

Ghostly Phallic:
For years, you all have been led to believe that there are no remaining phalluses, but there are three

(Kujichagulia looked around the cellar, a sliver of hope replaced the frown of her curled lips)

One in the deep East of Kampala
⠀⠀⠀⠀One, here, in the West of Afriq (*Gold Coast*)
⠀⠀⠀⠀⠀⠀One in *You*

Veiled Medusozoa:
In me…h…how? I am barren…
these fountains give life?

Ghostly Phallic:
You don't focus much, do you?
Your blood, is now that of our blood- all the phallic properties spring through you.
It won't take long for your physic to undergo drastic changes in androgen levels

Veiled Medusozoa:
So, will I be a male member, now?

Ghostly Phallic:
No, technically you would be considered asexual and
will have the ability to undergo fragmentation

Veiled Medusozoa:
I'll have to be amputated?

Ghostly Phallic:
I wouldn't think of it on such grotesque terms; your
body will be able to split and regenerate itself. Yes,
this will alter your physical being but it's never
permanent

Veiled Medusozoa:
It seems like a strenuous process on the body… how
are we to know how successful this can be, what if
this proves to compromise my physical being?

Ghostly Phallic:
You should know all too well the supernatural
uncertainties of our heritage. We are the
Medusozoans, it is in our nature, if properly
performed, to sustain. You've made it this far,
Kujichagulia…This veil is only your guise now, not
your being

Veiled Medusozoa:
My fate has chosen me

Ghostly Phallic:
Because you have re-activated your soul tie, we will
do much to guide you on your journey of re-
populating Meditron. On your journey, you must do
much to take care of yourself

(*The hallowed pits of the underground cave began to
crumble as male voices echoed screams around
Kujichagulia's temple. The earth beneath Kuji's feet
quaked, the walls cracked until the outside world
crept through large crevices. The floors separated
multi-directionally and so did Kuji. Screams of
ancestors swarmed cyclically until there was nothing
left but crumbled debris and an old map.
Kujichagulia, with careful hands, picked the map up
and instantly felt the elder phallic's vibrational voice.
She placed it in her side satchel next to the copper
chip retrieved from Xora's throat)*

You will find use for this very soon

***

(*Kujichagulia walked cautiously out of the prison and
searched for her mother*)

Veiled Medusozoa:
Mama!?

(*Pause*)
          Mama! You can come out now!
(*Pause*)

Where are you?

Elder Womb:
Shh...child, I'm over here! There are sirens approaching us from the East, we must move quickly

(*Elder Womb remained in a crouch, her head just above the standing blackberry bushes*)

It took you long enough, did you find anything?

(*Veiled Medusozoa removed the blood stained copper flash drives from their left boot*)

Where on Meditron did you find such a device?
Veiled Medusozoa:
I thought you would reactivate the portal after thirty minutes...

Elder Womb:
You know I wouldn't leave you behind, my love. I knew there was no cause for concern when you never whistled
Now, what information did you gather?

Veiled Medusozoa:
Do you remember Xora? Turns out she was the head coordinator of this Alphacorp site

Elder Womb:
We have lost our religion
You are not the womb who left me an hour ago—there's something different about you, I can smell it

Veiled Medusozoa:
I have too much to tell you Mama, but we must get off of this land and trail West, apparently there are five active fountains; one disguised as a Hue man in the Gold Coast

Elder Womb:
Hmph…it seems like we are constantly on the run, I am growing weary of this mission

Veiled Medusozoa:
Look into my eyes, mama, we will find salvation. The spirit of Dr. Nia-oh guided me whilst in the underground cell…from our conversation, I think there is refuge further north, past the Gold Coast

Elder Womb:
The Gold Coast? Look around you, baby, there is no refuge outside of the nature that is God

Veiled Medusozoa:
We must find this living phallus, I need to see him with my own eyes…this could be a beneficial partnership. Trust me, Queen Mother, Dr. Nia-oh would not lead us astray…

(Kuji, extended their arms toward the Elder Womb and embraced her tightly)

I think we should find shelter until we can solar charge tomorrow

Elder Womb:
Good thinking, my dear

(The Elder Womb shifted on her heels as if the earth shook beneath her, she clenched her womb and reached for her child to steady her)

Veiled Medusozoa:
Is it another spell?

Elder Womb:
I've made some findings of my own in the last few months

(The Elder Womb fell back to the ground and crossed her legs, straightened her spine and let her shoulders fall at ease. She hummed for ten minutes and motioned Kuji to hush)

"Theres another force with you, interfering our connection. Are you alright?

"They remind me of you; motherly and masculine. We are moving slightly South to get to a shuttle station."

(A loud high frequency pitch blared the Elder Womb's ears)

"We...g-...Wes-...Kampa-...Medi-"
"Citronella! Your signal is compromised, try adjusting yourself"

*(The ringing was joined by a brief bout of
static and Citronella's network disappeared)*

Veiled Medusozoa:
Mama, what's going on? Who were you talking to?

Elder Womb:
I was assigned a spiritual subject to guide, some
time ago

Veiled Medusozoa:
You are the officiating High Priestess of
Medusozoa in the absence of Baba, how could
someone give you orders?

Elder Womb:
Our multiverse is a lot more than space and time,
daughter

*(The word daughter slipped past Kujichagulia's
memory of what they had been before today)*

Veiled Medusozoa:
We are far enough from the prison camp, I must
show you some things I collected while there

*(Kuji slowed down and directed their mother off the
mud paved road and into an abandoned living
compound. There was no sign of free life in this part
of Meditron, everyone was considered an
indentured servant. Xora and her officials were in
the business of trading Medusozoans to neighboring
countries and planets for monetary gain. 20 of the*

*35 wombs who escaped with the Elder and Kuji,
decided that death was better than constantly living
in fear of their enslavement.
They found a small room to settle in, at least for a
few hours before going about their way)*

I found a copper disk in Xora's throat, here

Elder Womb:
For years, I told you that womb was troubled. She
didn't love herself to love you, baby

(*Mama's hands warmed the side of Kuji's face*)

Kujichagulia:
There is more…I met one of our male members, Dr.
Nia-oh his spirit spoke to me, though not in physical
form

(*a tear fell from Mama's left eye*)

My body is transitioning, Mama, into something I
believed outside of my capacity…but this feeling is-
is- rejuvenating

Elder Womb:
I sensed a foreign air about you post-return.

Kujichagulia:
Up until now, I hadn't noticed the true meaning
behind our culture, what it means to be a
Medusozoan…how we have innate ability to sustain
and reproduce from self

(the Elder Womb chuckled and squeezed her child tight with conviction. Her head dropped as she struggled to recount the memories of her loves)

Kujichagulia:
Theres a regenerative force within me that will allow me to reproduce asexually

Elder Womb:
You have what the ancestors call, poly-mor(pH+ism) [2]. Until now, I thought poly-morphic Medusozoans were just myths passed down from our ancestors. I haven't heard talk of nü life ceremonies since their extraction… 'Guess there's still hope in the future of our people

Kujichagulia:
I have already begun my transition, Dr. Nia-oh said it won't be long before I start shedding regenerative appendages

---

[2] Poly-mor(pH+ism) is a spin on polymorphism which refers to an organism's ability to regenerate. The characters pH+ and ism, represent loose measurements of acidity/alkalinity and its systemic nature

Cosma + Zaastria (*Lover-lude*)

Someone once mentioned that there were two
frequencies the ears could capture; that of the high
and that of the low; love and fear. It is hierarchical,
symptoms may include selective hearing. Selectivity,
a thing I suffer from; what with so many options. It is
hard to accept when something has been designed for
me.

"I could love you."

The revolution in us wanted to combat this
dichotomy because even in the quail of love, was the
shimmering undertone of war. Trying not to digress
back into binary, we created refugee camps. Two
bodies with enough lineage to germinate, were
composed from those walls.

"How could you bring your mouth to maneuver such
words?"

We are reckless and find it difficult to make
vulnerable a self we spent centuries digging from
overcrowded graves. Digging is synonymous to
pulling and reaching, both of these acts are retrieving
glory. Restitution.

"Because when I see you, no matter the dark, no
matter the light, I see the elder you. The wiser you.
Your body which is so consumed in spirit, that I
know time can only tell."

"Please do not blame this on time. Time has been the victim for far too long."

"Then let us accuse space for making us feel entitled to have more of it, when we need less."

Despite the expense of euro conditioning, the bodies without recollection of their past names, suffered from a divine unconsciousness. And in introducing themselves to one another with little words and with widened eyes, a physiopsychic void was created.

"So, what is it to be in love, when your soul already knows its existence?"

"It is to suspend yourself into the unknown and let it bring forth all the things you never you were keeping from yourself."

"Growth?"

"I only have words?"

"Then we must do much to plant them."

EXTENSION IV

Voyage
To
Meditron

It was thirty past midnight and the five were off trailing the woods in a paired file line, although Knowl always led the group, she stuck behind on careful trail duty, staying alert to nearing trouble. Cosma and Zaastria swayed with one another ahead of the Trillage.

"How did we find we?"
"Something in the body carried us"
"Can we truly measure this experience?"
"Have you felt dry ice become fiery enough to burn?"
"As sure as our sun signs ignite each other. So then... we are, really here?"
"Yes, but I would like to be there..."

Without touching Symptron Zaas' epidermis, Symptron Cosma calculated the energetic currents within Huemoon's body and noticed the tremor on shem's brow, and sent kiss waves

"There, do you feel it?" Zaas giggled just enough to cover her rosy cheeks.

"Hey, you two, cut that quasi love shit out and focus on the trail before you!" Knowl called out to the kitty lovers.

"We've got 7 more hours of walking to do, we don't even have enough copper to forge some hover fuel," Zaastria yelled.

"Even if we did have some copper, it wouldn't be enough for the whole trip," Va said.

"How does that correlate to annoying lust banter?" Knowl asked the two, rhetorically.

"It means, the least they can do for energy accumulation, is to exchange some kind of mutual vibration, Knowl, don't be a dung dealer," Kalic negotiated.

"I can't imagine being caged, love doesn't exist anymore. As survivors of the devolution, I thought you four would overstand," Knowl stated sharply, "instead, I wound up with two couples…"

"You're exactly the Symptron those mind feeders wanted to create. You try so hard to hate, to be numb," Cosma shoved xem's palm onto Knowl's pineal area. "How can you know all the right herbs to heal sickness and not the right thoughts to heal your mind?"

Knowl (*Lover-lude*)

Mind:

I knew love…had it linger on me like
mosquitos on sweet, sweaty skins. This love
was parasitic, it wanted me to water its soil,
to manicure its buds and barely nurture
mine; we never blossomed. Instead, we
spent hours tangled from root to crown
beckoning some spiritual motion to propel
us, we figured, if we could stare at one
another unflinchingly, we would see truth.

"It takes more than words, child, we've got
to walk the walk too," an elder disclosed to
me.

We hardly walked together, there were more
theories than miles. I hadn't much
experience to compare love to, when it did
find me, I was disengaged.

They were brown, had melanin drip neither
with the glimmer of gold, nor with the sweet
of honey, rather with the tint of burgundy
aged blood sacrificed on thirsty soil. They
fertilized and knew that trauma was only
relative to function.

"What you gon' do with it when it finds
you?" elder asked me.

I wanted to answer, "be selfless, and let it
slip between my fingers so that some residue
would still stick to me and the rest, left to
the earth…so this soul would know how
infinite this love could be," instead I settled
for, "whisper all my prior flaws in their ear
and how I've changed."
Humility dripped across my mind.

***

The Trillage stopped to catch their breaths. There
were thick blankets of smog covering the air, each of
them covered their faces with ready-made masks of
cloth and leaves. Knowl could only stare to the stars
and reflect on the validity of their thoughts.

"If we don't get to clear oxygen soon, our thought
processors will become clouded and we won't be
able to gauge oncoming threats while journeying,"
Va reminded the group.

"We passed a *Re-Up-A-Center* sign a few klicks
back, we can find anything for the road there. Usually
wherever there's a market, there's a Hover Shuttle
Station," Zaastria said.

As the Trillage each dug around in their clothing
articles for loose metals, three young looking hues
approached them.

"Looks like we've found ourselves 5 symps!" one of
the more confident straggly ones called to the others.

"Now, I'm not too sure we've seen your faces 'round these parts before. Clint, you seen this type folk hoverin' our town?"

"No sign of 'em Trout, they look to me like some copper pickin' jokers…Say, are y'all lost? You aint heard of the Space-portation Clause?" Clint inquired.

"Now, now kinfolk, don't go spillin' spells…See we classier then that. Now the law requires we kill your kind cold copper if y'ever trespass the Symptron-hue (Sh) border… Bern, sho'em the platinum stakes," Trout advised the third hue. Bern pulled back his trench-coat and unveiled five sleek platinum spear heads.

"We aren't looking for conflict with you hues, me and my squad are just trying to cross the border to get further south," Kalic interjected. "We don't have weapons and we barely have goods."

"That's up to us to decide… Bern and Clint, go fetch their carriers."

There was a low muffled sound nearing the group, Knowl taps her forehead to activate her third-dreyeve and checked the real time GPS tracker. A tiny red dot surfaced on the map and reached closer to where they were standing by the second.

"Check your drives," Knowl cautioned the Trillage. All of them began checking their third-dreyeve in sequence and darted scheming eyes at one another.

Bern and Clint fumbled around in the Trillage's pockets and belongings

"Who told y'all to talk and what y'all staring at?" Trout demanded.

"Look like they plottin' Trout," Bern pointed toward the oncoming Hover Shuttle.

"Quick! Use all of the hover fuel you have left to catch that shuttle!" Knowl coached the rest of the Trillage. Each of them quickly ran toward the shuttle and within seconds were able to catch flight above the ground. The straggly hues cursing at the Trillage launched their spears, one of them caught the back of Zaas' neck.

"Cosm-!" Zaas belched and plummeted onto the earth rolling, "keep going!" she yelled to the Trillage who were already climbing atop the shuttle. Only Cosma came to her rescue, extending her hand.

"Reach!   Zaas! Reach!" she strained. After almost falling back to earth's surface, Cosma grabbed a hold of Zaastria's arm and attempted to drag her back toward the Hover Shuttle, but Clint desperately held onto her leg. Zaastria smashed his hand with her left foot and watched the brainwashed terrorist roll helplessly on the jagged surface. Cosma, faintly carrying along Zaas, reached the rest of the Trillage who were waiting on the ceiling of the Hover Shuttle.

"We need firearms," Va said satirically, the rest of them affirmed the suggestion, in skeptical chorus.

Hover Shuttle Operator:
(*over a speaker*)

I'm stopping the shuttle, you all must board properly 5...4...3...

(The Trillage slowly climb down from the roof and entered through the automatic door)

That'll be 50 copper pieces

(The Trillage all look around at one another, Knowl reaches in her pocket and rummages up five coppers and takes it to the operator)

Hover Shuttle Operator:
This'll only get y'all to Meditron

Knowl:
Perfect...how far is Meditron from the Gold Coast station?

Hover Shuttle Operator:
What you want with Meditron? It's been a ghost town for at least a decade

Knowl:
Trying to find some indixene tribe members for "research"

Hover Shuttle Operator:
Oh, I see…well uhh, it's a ways on foot- least three
days without hover fuel

Knowl:
Say, you don't seem to be a hue or a Symptron; you
have no pineal implant or copper extremities…

Hover Shuttle Operator:
Yea, I'm still among what's left of the human race,
I'm working a life sentence debt

(the operator stared off into the distance)

I've said enough, the MFG have tracking devices all
over this Hover Shuttle…but I guess I have nothing
else to lose…

(Operator chuckles)

Knowl:
This system is shit   *(long pause)*   …say… *(brief
pause)* would you mind spotting us some

*(Knowl gestured to the heels of her feet for hover
fuel)*

We don't have much copper left and we really need
to get there…

Hover Shuttle Operator:
I usually don't liken to strangers but I can see
something in your eyes- we will be nearing the
Meditron stop in a half hour, Ill spot you then

Knowl:
With gratitude sir, by the way, what's your identifier?
Hover Shuttle Operator:
I'm 5973, but in the ethers, bodies refer to me as
Ghost 97

Knowl:
Ghost 97, you have been most spirited, you think we
can exchange frequencies, we might need someone
like you for the future

(*the Operator pulled over for a brief second and
raised his eyes to meet Knowls'- they spent a few eye
blinks exchanging third-dreyeve data*)

Hover Shuttle Operator:
Now, enjoy some moments of rest and take a seat,
you'll know when we are there, you'll be able to
smell it

(*Knowl hovered back to the seating area and found
the rest of the resting. Knowl brought a particular
force that made Valerian's body shift between Kalic's
hold. Knowl huffed and plopped on the seat, looking
outside the window to an indigo blue draped natively
on the trees. Stars talked and gleamed truths. In that
moment, Knowl felt some togetherness, a ping of
electricity revived their heart. Hours passed*)

Hover Shuttle Operator:
(*over loud speaker*)

This is the Meditron Station

(*Pause*)

I repeat, this is the Meditron Station, all passengers peering to exit here or make a transfer please get off, this is the Meditron Station

(*As the Trillage exit the Hover Shuttle, Knowl lags behind and goes up to the Operator*)

Knowl:
Thank you again for the ride and…well, y'know…

Ghost 97:
No problem, there's enough for all five of you, to last a while

(*the Operator tossed a bulky bag of cubes to Knowl*)

Be sure to keep your stinkers about you, this place is a cesspool, lotta co-zombs here, and they'd do anything to get their receptors on some fuel

(As *the Trillage wander off the Hover Shuttle and into the striking heat of Meditron, Ghost 97 called out to Knowl*)

Whatever you do, STAY WOKE and STAY STRAPPED! There's a Re-Up-A-Center 50 klicks

south from an abandoned Alphacorp church, you will
find firearms there

(*The Trillage stepped off the hover shuttle and into
the dense smog of twilight. All of them activated their
night sensors and prepared for worldly uncertainties;
life*)

Cosma:
Did that guy seem a little off his jets?

(*Nervous laughter skipped among the Trillage. Kalic
radiated Knowl's internal waist wallet with his third
optical scanner, almost sizing them up*)

Kalic:
Not in the least but I did see him toss Knowl a
package, what do you have there?

Knowl:
I was going to equip us, once a common wave of
fatigue fell over the group. But since you're so
pressed to know, (*Knowl clicked their tongue at
Kalic*) the shuttle operator spotted us some hover fuel
to last a few days

Va:
Sweet come up, Knowl

Zaas:
Yea, I guess you still know how to be empathetic
after all

(Zaas teased while holding onto Cosma's arm. Knowl passed out four hover packs to each Trillage member, xem was left with only two…)

Knowl:
We cannot use these packs until we've exhausted our own hover fuel and cannot find time to solar charge! I repeat, we cannot use these for the fuck of it!

(Hyper-melanated bodies shape shifted with their environment. The Trillage crawled, walked, ran, hovered and flew in consecutive increments from sunrise to sundown. Everyone was exhausted, dry sweat crusts formed around the crevices of their faces and their bodies were covered in red earth. They decided to rest for a few hours, Kalic and Cosma dug into the rich earth to bathe themselves with the damp soil for cooling purposes. After covering her face with the earth, Va addressed the Trillage)

Va:
I think it's safe to say, we can use some hover fuel for the next bout…Are we even close?

Knowl:
According to my navigation system, without hover fuel, we have a remaining 53 hours of travel time

Zaas:
And with hover fuel?

Knowl:
Four hours

Kalic:
And you've known (*struggling between pants*) this entire time! We need to-

Knowl:
We need to decide if we are going to rest for the night or continue the journey. Either way, we need to keep walking, to reach the Re-Up-A-Center, we need protection

Va:
There have been no threatening signs yet

Knowl:
That's the nerve-racking part, theres gotta be some travelers, cola-zombs or something around here

Cosma:
Knowl's right, it's been too quiet. We might be better off trekking without hover fuel until we reach the re-up spot...all in favor yell, "Ay!"

(*The other three looked around at one another in dismay and yelled, "Ay!" The Trillage trudged for three hours until they reached an abandoned church. The group slowed down and took in the eerie feeling that rushed over their copper stained skins, the church hunched over them*)

Kalic:
I don't know about you all, but I'm beat

Va:
We need to activate our night vision and walk closely
together to avoid anyone getting snatched off guard

(*Kalic clung to Va tighter. As the Trillage walked
cautiously pass the church, a loud thud and shrieks of
bird chatter escaped its pulpited tabernacle. The
cyclicity of historical fears looped as they stared into
the present unknown*)

Knowl:
We only have a few more yards to go…but
something is off…

(*In the abandoned Alphacorp church, some local
MFGs were hiding out, awaiting the groups arrival.
The gang received word that a suspicious group of
Symptrons were headed to Meditron*)

> "We've got eyes on them officer," said one
> of the MFGs.
> "Whatever you do, don't make yourselves
> known until they reach neutral
> destination…do you copy?"
> "Yes, 5973, copy."

Knowl:
Do you all still have some copper fare?

(*the group haphazardly affirmed*)

We need to buy some weaponry, the shuttle operator said there're plenty of cola-zombs out here

Zaas:
You two sure were talking about a lot, how do you know he wasn't for the MFGs?

Knowl:
He wasn't, just a regular being…Alright, we don't have much time, let's get what we need so we can hover for a few hours

(The Trillage could now see the large green fluorescent Re-Up-A-Center sign in plain sight, they seemed to have a rush of energy and got there in a few eye-blinks. They each took shopping turns in pairs so three of them could stand guard outside. Kalic managed to shoplift a few buck steel blades for Va and him, Zaas bought a 9mm Caliber, Cosma bought a Glock 40 and Knowl talked the shop manager into giving her a good deal on a Smith and Wesson rifle. Altogether they had 350 rounds of ammunition. As the Trillage reconvened outside of the center, they each inserted a hover fuel pack into the soles of their feet. While hovering, everyone followed Knowl since they knew where the indixene land was. Three hours later, Va pointed out two specs to the rest of the Trillage)

Va:
Hey, do y'all see those two beams radiating in the distance? We haven't seen a living thing in over 1700 eye-blinks!

Kalic:
Oh snap! you're right…

Cosma:
Let's check them out…remember, keep a low profile!

Knowl:
… unless they have information

***

(The Trillage made sure to hover in the distance to avoid startling the two wanderers. As both parties neared, the Trillage kept their hands in plain sight. A light encircled all of them)

Knowl:
Greetings, we were hovering and couldn't help but notice that you two have been the only hues we've seen coming from the direction we're headed…

(Kalic waited a while for one of the wanderers to speak)

Veiled Medusozoa:

(Veiled Medusozoa looked to their mother and spoke in foreign tongue, the mother's guard seemed to drop and she smiled at the Trillage)

Forgive us, our city speech is not well. My name is Kujichagulia and this is Mama.

(Veiled Medusozoa did not shake any of their hands, instead, placed xem's palm in front of their faces to read them)

In our religion, we read beings with our palms...you mentioned that you are headed in the direction we came, right?

Knowl:
Yes, we are trying to find some indixene members of Meditron

(Kujichagulia translated to the Elder Womb and they both chuckled at this)

Veiled Medusozoa:
It seems the universe has provided

(xem lifted their hands to the eggplant sky)

We are of the indixene hues...why are you looking for us?

(Knowl took a few steps back and reached into their side satchel for their collective findings)

Knowl:
We are grateful for this connection. Please accept these offering; yam seeds to nurture, mugwort to cleanse, jasmine to enliven, chamomile to soothe.

(Kalic dug into his jacket and presented five seeded mangos, skin soft and leathery. The Elder Womb

smirked and summoned the group near. Everyone introduced themselves. The collective of interplanetary hues settled amongst a leafy patch of soil outside a wooden shed just 500 clicks of the abandoned church)

Zaas:
If you don't mind my asking, why were you all leaving Meditron?

Veiled Medusozoa:
Questions are welcomed. See, we come from the most southern point of Meditron.

(they all started walking west off the trail)

The Alphacorps down there are ruthless; infiltrated our land seven years ago and imprisoned all of our men underground…the spirits have implanted a mission in only a few of us

Cosma:
We found a flash drive with your tribes' language embedded in the text…we need help translating the message

(out of nowhere, Kalic's right pant leg started to throb, he dug into his pocket and felt heat radiating from the three copper keys. The Veiled Medusozoa spoke to their mother, the Elder Womb shook her head and pointed to the sky)

Veiled Medusozoa:
Even the moon is growing tired, we should find shelter

(the Veiled Medusozoa walked over to Kalic and touched his heart and whispered in his right ear)

You are hiding information from your tribe, do not be afraid to share the gifts given to you, we know the doors they open

Va:
Uhm… what's going on?

(a part of her womanhood stung with jealousy)

Veiled Medusozoa:
We, too, have come upon a few copper chips. Of course, if either one of us tried to read the encrypted language, we could damage the entire drive with our electrical force

(Kujichagulia took off their hijab)

Zaas:
Whoa, when you said indixene, I had no clue you meant the Medusozoa tribe

Knowl:
I can speak for all of us when I say, we are truly blessed to be in the presence of demigods…but what do you mean, Kalic is hiding something from us?

Kalic:
Kujichagulia is right

(*he wiped any impending sweat on his brow before continuing*)

before Master One died, he gave me three copper keys. I have been having inner visions for a few months now, I think they are his memories...

Va:
Months...?

Kalic:
The day of his death, I went back to his office and found Beta-medics prepping his burnt body onto a stretcher, I disguised myself as a Beta-medic to get inside where his body was...there were three tiny flash drives shoved up his anal cavity...I believe the keys and flash drives correspond with one another but I have no clue how to access them...when Zaas found the copper drive in the forest that day, I knew they were all pieces to the same puzzle

(*Kalic looked around at the Trillage who were all still processing the new information, he turned to the Veiled Medusozoa and the Elder Womb and extended his findings. The Veiled Medusozoa hovered over the objects with their palms and tears fell*)

Veiled Medusozoa:
These are all pieces of evidence the Alphacorp took on the Medusozoan people and theories they were

unable to prove…Kalic, for over a year, you have been holding the keys to what separates hue from man; space-portation…
These three keys represent portals for the lower world, higher world and the fountains

Knowl:
What is all of this? What is space-portation?
(*the Elder Womb spoke in their language*)

Cosma:
That fool hours back, along with his squad mentioned something about space-portation laws but-

Zaas:
They were obviously some copper-pickin' scoundrels with nothing better to do than harass us. Fear is see through.

(*The Elder Womb spoke in her foreign tongue, repeated, 'Sc-He-Me[3],' and smiled openly at Kalic*)

Veiled Medusozoa:
Mama says that before the Alphacorp came to many rich lands cross planets and countries, many indixene polyviduals were aware of space and time travel…however, once the Alphacorps came, ancestors and indixene persons were forced to hide their spiritual crafts.

---

[3] *Sc*-> Sekh | *He*-> Heru(t) | *Me*-> Met (flip) Sekhmet->Sun Goddess of Healing and War | Heru(t)-> Sky God of Sun and Moon

(the Elder Womb spoke once more in their language and made gestures to the earth and moon)

space-portation is more than hovering and travelling through hover portals…space-portation allows those who are spiritually inclined to tap into planes greater than the physical spatial realm. Ancestors and indixene members are able to go back and forward in time. Those before us knew of life on the moon and sun…Space-portation allows those who are blessed, a way to live with the dead and those who have yet to live…

(the Elder Womb chuckled and motioned her hand to her mouth)

Mama says to pick up your jaws, why else do you think they came to every rich land? To gain insight.

(The three copper keys continued to radiate heat in Kalic's hands and started glowing a red hue. The MFGs managed to follow the Trillage for their entire journey, preserving their disguise behind the tall forest trees)

> **MFG 2:**
> You think we should contact Ghost to update him on the two Medusozoas?
> **MFG 1:**
> Na, let's hold off until we find some additional information

Zaas:
Your elder mentioned that there were three levels to space-portation; the lower-world, the higher-world and the fountains. What does each level mean?

Veiled Womb:
The lower-world consists of the peoples who are stuck in the grey area of life's essence
Knowl:
The people who were unable to fulfill their testimony, or who completely went against universal will...

(*Knowl finished Kujichagulia's statement*)

Veiled Medusozoa:
You have done half of your homework. The lower-world is also a means of salvation. Hues undergo a series of tests to determine the growth of their choices and conduct. We can always evolve from our slumber.

Knowl:
Learning is only third of the battle...

Va:
So, what about the higher-world and the fountains?

Veiled Medusozoa:
The higher world is much like-

(The Trillage and Medusozoans were interrupted by an abrasive force)

MFG 1:
Well what the fuck do we have here?

MFG 2:
A group of exiles, eh? What's in your hands?

(Both MFGs reached for their firearms but before they could pull their triggers, the Veiled Medusozoa and Elder Womb removed their head dresses and revealed their glowing scars and tentacles. As the two Medusozoans were conjuring electrical force from the universe, Cosma, Zaas and Knowl assembled their guns and shot at the MFGs, only Knowl's submachine gun pierced MFG 2s left shoulder)

MFG 2:
You piece of sh-!

(MFG 2 fired his trifle letting off a series of stray bullets, the Elder Womb with her long tentacles swayed each of them from her direction and watched the bullets ricochet. She then sent electric currents to MFG 2 and his body convulsed rhythmically until he slowly fell to the earth. One of the stray bullets stopped near Kalic's abdomen; instead of piercing through his flesh, the bullet hovered over his skin and fell. He looked around to see if there were any witnesses to this miracle but found Va hurdled toward the ground, holding the center of her chest as blood seeped through her hands)

Kalic:
Valerian!

(*Kalic crouched to her level and examined the wound*)

MFG 2:
89!

(*in a whisper*)

call for backup! Now! Agent 89! Lookou-

(*Kuji grabbed MFG 1 by the neck with her tentacles and electrocuted him for several eye blinks until there were burn marks around his collar. The two MFGs lied helplessly on the grass and within moments, their bodies began to disintegrate into grey static. The Trillage and Medusozoans all heaved and looked around to make sure there were no more MFGs lurking in the shadows. Kalic's body began to radiate*)

Kalic:
Valerian is injured

(*The group hover around Valerian*)

Veiled Medusozoa:
You, too, are a healer…

(*The elder's words tickled Kalic's fingertips. Kalic looked to his hands and then at Va. The Elder Womb embodied him and puppeteered him closer to Valerian's wound. Kujichagulia translated for her mother)*

Veiled Medusozoa:
Rub your hands together to create a current from your energetic field and slowly hover them over the affected area.

(Kalic hovered over Valerians wound and practiced multiple deep breaths. A static wind prickled her numb skin until she could feel again. Her flesh hardened and the shot scabbed over. Valerian's irritated skin was back to its browned hue in no time)

Elder Womb:
Scheme!

(she pointed to her heart and mind at the same time)

Veiled Medusozoa:
It is time to activate the higher world's door Kalic

Kalic:
But...I...I don't know how? You didn't tell us anything about the higher-world or its function

Veiled Medusozoa:
You were given the keys for a reason, Master One knew your power, you must unlock the doors one at a time

(*Kalic closed his eyes for a few moments and thought of Master One…What do you want me to do, please Master One…please guide me. Kalic waited and stirred in his emotions*)

The activation of the lower world portal is far easier than you imagine

(*Kujichagulia looked to mama and they both smirked in knowing*)

It is this immediate experience,

(*they pointed to the tribe's kin and circled the air in front of them*)

both lived and shared, that create the multitude of our life lessons

Valerian:
It seems like a never ending journey

Veiled Medusozoa:
Once our trials have been conditioned and weighed against universal laws, we advance in assignment

The higher-world portal requires those who activate it, a keener endurance

Cosma:
Do the Fountains act as a controlling unit of the worlds?

Veiled Medusozoa:
The Fountains are an energy transmitter, they are omni-functional and mostly used as a healing hub to upkeep our genepool

(the Elder Womb noticed the uncertainty tilt across their faces)

Elder Womb:
Medusozoans are amongst the oldest living species. We did not always have our powers, it took generations of adaptation and conditioning...eventually, our people could communicate with other forces...the learning hardly ever stops. Time is sacred young hue, call upon your loved one

Kalic:
How?

Elder Womb:
Look within

(Kalic's eyes winced as he tried to mull over lingering emotions he spent 500 days suppressing. His mind raced anxiously until a familiar voice cradled his heart)

      Master One's Spirit:
      I've waited for you to call on me, boy
      So, you've found your ancestors, huh?

Kalic:
Wh-What do you mean, my ancestors?

> **Master One's Spirit:**
> You weren't abandoned as an infant. You
> are the last male Medusozoan… haven't you
> ever questioned the scars on your back?

Kalic:
Yea, but I thought they were just from child abuse,
or-

> **Master One's Spirit:**
> You are Baba Umoja's last son. Shortly after
> the government began extracting male
> Medusozoans, he made reproductive
> arrangements with another woman and
> advised her to leave Meditron. Your father
> knew of the troubles plaguing his home…he
> knew this day would come.

Kalic:
How do you know all of this?

> **Master One's Spirit:**
> Umoja and I became closer during the latter
> years of his life. Your biological mother
> thought it best to place you in the care of
> another family who had no ties to the
> Medusozoan tribe. You were able to pass the
> randomized Alphacorp mental tests without
> knowledge of your ancestry.

Kalic:
Instead, I was abused emotionally, mentally and physically…had to walk around lost and vulnerable in my skin.

(The branches on his back glowed)

Do you know how it feels to be nameless, to have foreign blood coursing through your veins?

> **Master One's Spirit:**
> I understand your angst, Kalic. You were 3689 just 7 months ago! I know how it feels to be nameless, to be deduced to a numeric sequence in the guise of a group who enslaved me. Look around you, you're not alone. Redirect your daddy issues into something practical…
>
> Show them…Kujichagulia and Mama
> They will help you activate your true self

(Master One's spirit vanished from Kalic's inner vision and he stood limp at the center of all of them. He removed his shirt from over his head, still frowning at the bitter taste Master One left in his mouth, his tongue bitten and bloodied. Words, Words. He asked the group to look at his scars)

Kalic:
Do these make sense to you?

(The Veiled Medusozoa chuckled aloud and called to their mother)

Veiled Medusozoa:
You were a lot closer than I imagined. Mama look at his markings

(the Elder Womb traced Kalic's back with her hands, his scars glowed a maroon, his posture seemed to elongate and tentacles formed in place of his unkempt beard. A thump of familiarity knocked the elder into a stale memory of her late husband)

Elder Womb:
I should have known from the way your eyes seem to stretch into souls
(She held her index fingers at the base of his eye lids as tears fell from her own)

Kalic:
Is this really who I am now?

Veiled Medusozoa:
You are salvation, Kalic

(The words drummed at Kalic's sternum and tried to direct themselves from his clenched vocal chords)

Kalic:
H-how do we get to the higher world?

Elder Womb:
You must breathe intentionally. Deep breaths are a
catalyst in generating our life force.

(*Kalic stared at the tentacles stretched before his
arms and shook uncontrollably. Va sobbed into her
palms, Kalic reached over and pulled her closer. The
tentacles from his back wrapped around her body
and instead of electrocuting her, the copper of her
skin radiated with flushes of red*)

Kalic:
I'm still the same Kalic, Va…

Va:
…I know

(*Valerian hugged him unbothered by the burning
surge inside her…the rest of the Trillage were stuck,
speechless. Out of nowhere, the Elder Womb
screamed for dear life and held onto her womb*)

Veiled Medusozoa:
My mother is what you call a Queen Mother, in our
country…she is a high priestess and sole counsel for
many of the wombs in our tribe; sometimes she gets
visions and must communicate cross space

(*Kuji waved to deflect their attention*)

Knowl:
Will she be alright?

(Knowl felt a shiver fly from their stomach and settled on the top of their loin)

Elder Womb:
I'll be fine

(The Elder Womb smiled as she sensed the tickle of Knowl's womb. She looked to her child in a weird cosmic knowing and back at the Symptron)

We must breathe as a collective force; deeply, letting our bellies expand; breathing in our intentions; exhaling any blockage hindering our growth. Once we reach unison, our minds and bodies will feel different, we will be in direct unit with one another. For some, this will be a burden, for you have fought an entire life to hold onto a piece of your prescribed self. Sadly, we must unlearn the identities given to us, if we want to advance as a collective. Do you all understand the fate that has chosen you?

(Everyone bowed their heads skeptically in agreement. They created a cypher and joined arms, each touching one another's backs. The collective took 7 deep breaths and a gust of wind formed in the middle of their cypher.

Gravel and earth matter swirled with a synchronic upward pull and a winding light-field beamed down on each being)

Veiled Medusozoa:
It is happening…do not fear the cold creeping on
your skin. We are adjusting to a heightened force.
When we arrive, keep quiet, wait for mama to speak
peace unto the ancestors

*(The gusting wind evolved into a frenzied whirl, the
Trillage and indixenes surrendered their firm plant
on the ground and allowed themselves to be swept
into black light.* The gravel continued to rattle
upward as the Trillage and Medusozoans slowly
evaporated; only a static essence trailed toward the
sky.

*The pitch black consumed their bodies into individual
space bubbles as they ascended. The experience was
comparative to a turbulent plane. While in spatial
flight, each of them received inner visions and
reflected on their journeys)*

Kalic:
Somehow this space travel was beginning to make
me feel all the things I have been suppressing for two
years; before the devolution, before the Trillage,
before the indixenes. It took some time for me to
notice that the benign lump I always felt at the core
of my throat was guilt. There was so much
information circling amuck inside of me, so much
angst at not speaking my truth. No one told me the
exact costs of grieving, how I have to give a little
piece of myself every time I think, hear, see, smell of
him. Thrush sits atop my tongue, housing bacteria,

the lies creep out without my knowing…until it
becomes ritual, becomes necessary.
I never got a chance to get over One, he had left me
with so much information, never the evidence I truly
needed. I bit my lower lip, trying to remember those
feelings from the island. There were always a few
details from our joint memories that I seemed to
forget and remember at invasive times; when making
love to Va, how my hands grow slick with each grip
on her; a film of impermanence, another guilt to live
with.

A   I   R

Valerian:
I stand erected in confidence, slowly walking to the
horizon of the ocean. Waves wash their many lives
on me, my body chooses to retain the ones I've
known, the ones who've managed to stay. I keep
walking, the water covers my entire diaphragm, the
pull from the ocean bed growing deeper, my neck
stretching further, trying to breathe. Quick sand,
       steady   sink
I gulp this grit and continue to grin, bare, lick his
wounds when he cries. I am more mother than
woman, than lover. Ye, Ma, Ya. Stuck saving and
nurturing, never realizing how many times I've
sacrificed myself to drown, I've adapted gills;
breathing underwater for so long.

E   A   R   T   H

Cosma:
It is an act of revolution to love someone during
chaos. I can no longer hide from myself, from my

lover; she sees everything. We navigate struggle with the learned ease of pronouncing our names.

W   I   N   D

Zaastria:
We queer lovers got ism draped across our skin like firearms; this heart, a bullet to the hetero-normative system.   Fists up,   We shoot,   Hearts Up, We ready for war, do not mistake this need to defend, for hate…this is the most authentic love there is, that of sustaining a family unit. Brick to mortar, nail to wood. We have enough ancestors to fuel this mission, that of reconstructing our wealth. More than disposable paper unbacked by minerals and metals. We too copper to throw loose change. Pennies, are generational heirlooms to provoke thought, I take it a step closer and tape them to my mind and heart; igniting a frequency in this tech-advanced age, the only thing keeping me grounded, aside from the rhythm in her sway.

F   I   R   E

Knowl:
A green tint covered my eyes, knees shuffled in corn husks. Presence is near. Somehow, I am looking at myself from a higher vantage point, an electric string connects me to Kuji. We have yet to go over pronouns, but their energy jumps like the flame of a candle between feminine and masculine energies. Another string trails off far beyond my perception and I wonder who is on the other end.

A   I   R

Elder Womb:
Where are you, Citronella? Once we settle into the higher world, time will only accelerate. You are the missing key.

E   A   R   T   H

Veiled Medusozoa:
Dr. Nia-oh's words swam in fragments inside my mind, along with severed limbs. Impermanence a happening that results in infinitude; an everlasting endurance. In doer, open doors. Found.at.ion…she, we be, he, us climbing. Procure. Heal. We abundant. Reshape. Reconstruct. Restore.

W   I   N   D

(An immediate force burst their space bubbles and the collective smacked against a sporous foundation that reacted to each of their falls. Sprung forward in heat. Spirits roamed around them wearing only bronze and copper; trace minerals, woven tapestries of the earth, built upon similar properties)

Elder Womb:
Lord, Mother, Father, Creator, Most High, Most Low, Most Present… We come to you grateful for all that you have done, are doing and will do. We come to you ill prepared with truth in our hearts and memories on our tongues. We are your agents, use us.

(A meditative voice welcomed them into their shared cognitive reality)

"You are among the few who have made it
to the defining level," a knowing voice
informed them.

"It is here, in the mind, that you will activate
your fountains. It seems there are still truths
that need to unveil themselves," a black light
hovered over the group.

The Elder Womb planted herself firmly in an upright
posture and as if on cue, shared her research with the
group. "Up until a few days ago, our existence was
compromised," she looked to Kalic and her child
before resuming. "You have a sibling, Kuji, who if
under the proper guidance, can become far more
powerful than you and I combined."

The Veiled Medusozoan looked to their mother in
confusion, "what about the young woman you've
been communicating with tele-vaginally? How long
have you known about both of them?"
"I've been following her ever since she was born. As
an acting priestess, I was advised to monitor her
growth and guide her to us. Unfortunately, there was
some resistance during her upbringing and I lost
connection with her for almost fifteen years. I only
learned of Kalic when we all crossed paths in
Meditron."

"Why couldn't you just teleport to both of their
locations and bring them to the higher-world?" Kuji
asked their mother.

"Child, if it were that easy, we would not be an
extinct race," the weight of her emotions caused her
to slump forward, "your father thought he was doing
our people a service by impregnating a womb cross
planets in time before the complete infiltration of
Alphacorp. I was never able to get clarity or closure
from Umoja before his capture. Somehow there is a
bridge between Citronella and Kalic...

Years after our communication was compromised,
Citronella found me during a chemically induced
subconscious state. It's taken quite some time to get
her reacquainted with the notion of our supernatural
force, imagine the patience needed to teach her of our
complexities," the Elder Womb circled her eyes in
the direction of the present ancestor.

> "You've done what you could, though your
> main objective was to deliver Citronella to
> her people once she was conscious of her
> gifts...bearing this in soul, you have not
> completed your mission. Fortunately for
> your sake, the moment you reunited with her
> total mind and body-being, we were able to
> track her location through sensory responses
> of her surroundings.

> We ejected an agent into her current world,
> who are among the few to withstand an
> intense series of testing. The other ancestors
> are quite confident in our agent's
> competence to deliver the seed but we'll
> need you on standby."

"Gracefully," the Elder Womb responded.

"Very well, then, you mus-"

Suddenly, the Elder Womb screamed excruciatingly until she was forced to the cloudy earth beneath her. A fast dry heave accelerated her breathing as she clenched the center of her chest, "it's, it's her!"

> "Try your hardest to stay connected with her, our agent's network is weak."

The Elder Womb breathed deeply until the rhythm of her breath became vibrations against the ear drums of the Trillage.

"Body...Body! Come in," she twisted her arms around her core and rocked back and forth until a pleasure filled rush breezed over her.

> "Nostalgia, my signal isn't strong, we may disconnect at any moment."

"Where are you?"

(The ancestor massaged her temples in cyclic motion and gently hummed. The stronger the Elder Womb's connection to Citronella grew, the clearer the ancestor could sense the subject's immediate environment)

> "In transit, as far away as possible from the camp," Citronella's voice shook.

"Now is the time to tap into your essence, black, you are the last fountain we need to activate our collective consciousness," the Elder Womb momentarily broke tele-vaginal connection to study the ancestor's eyes.

The pain grew heavier in the Elder Womb's gut as she tried to salvage their weak signal.

"Don't strain yourself, I've gotten enough," as the ancestor came nearer to the group, the purple tint cleared into a warm yellow light. The Trillage looked around with eyes squinted as if they were newborns, post womb, unto the world.

"Where is she?" The Elder Womb asked with bowed eyes.

> "Akuafiama, you are on a need to know access, lest your findings permit otherwise. We value you your ethic but time is precious."

The ancestor floated before the group.

> "This will be your temporary home for the evening. You will need all the rest you can get before embarking on your collective mission. There are provisions and toiletries in each of your respective capsules. Be sure to follow the directions and ingest everything properly. You will be suspended into the lower-world to resume your collective pursuit. All appliances have dial-

tone capability, any of your queries before suspension can be answered by a higher-world representative."

The ancestor's spirit evaporated throughout the neighboring air. The Trillage and Medusozoans looked to each other, defeat settled on their faces as they walked to their domains.

"Nearly 30 years to get to the beginning, HA!" Knowl cackled.

"I think we should sync dreyeves before we depart," Valerian looked to the two indixenes, "who knows if all of us will be evacuated at the same location."

The five hovered in a cypher, arms wrapped around the other and focused on their spiritual energy exchange. A holographic string wove from one hue to the next, they opened their eyes and followed the remnants of energy to their partners. As the string evaporated, an aura field sculpted the group into a half crescent. Kuji's eyes traveled to Knowls', who awaited their gaze. A rush of fire seared the pit of their stomachs.

After-Thoughts

MindFeeder+ Restoration, introduces a multiverse of queer, persons of hue. Each character is wrapped in nuance and must figure out their connective tissue. This story sets the tone for a larger series of said persons and how they navigate systemic structures, as a collective.

Readers are encouraged to pay attention to the tense and voice changes throughout the text, as they denote the relativity of space and time travel.

Questions for the reader:

What is power, how is it attained in this body of work?

What does it mean to be marginalized?

How does language construct the way people claim space in the world?

When will the oppressed/repressed groups be encouraged to successfully mobilize?

To continue the dialogue and build, contact the author at dvntphnk@gmail.com or @dvntphnk on Instagram